DREAMS

OF

FREEDOM

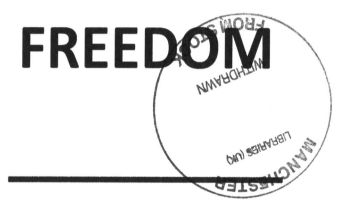

A Collection of Jamaican Short Stories

Linford Sweeney

Dreams of Freedom

Dreams of Freedom

In association with

.

Dreams of Freedom

Published in London by Peaches Publications, 2016.
www.peachespublications.weebly.com

The moral right of the author has been asserted.

British Library Cataloguing in Publication Data: A catalogue record for this book is available from the British Library.

ISBN: 978-1-326-75371-9

Book cover design: Tyalin Art, Manchester, UK

Typesetter: Winsome Duncan.

Dreams of Freedom

Contents

Dreams of Freedom

Dedication

———————

To my mother, Rettynellar, who started me on this incredulous
journey into understanding and researching my history and
ancestry – knowledge and experiences that have shaped, excited,
enthused and challenged me to dream and achieve.

Acknowledgements

I want to acknowledge some truly supportive people in my life. To my mother, Rettynellar, you were always there and gave me my keen interest in family and history; and my father, Renford, who gave me a love for telling stories. To my secondary school English teacher, Linda Horsfield, who inspired me to write; and to Whit Stennett, who became my 'informal mentor' and played a pivotal role in shaping the man within during my young adult life. To Valerie Hutchinson-Morgan who has been a motivational rock, designer of the book's mesmerising cover, and impromptu proofreader; and Julia McManus, an indomitable spirit and special friend, whose financial support was crucial to my travel to Jamaica and writing this book.

To my family, you all have a special place in my heart; particularly my wife Marjorie, daughters Angeli and Rosita, sisters Geniver, Dawn and Pansy, brother Horace, and numerous other family members here, who are too numerous to mention, but they know who you are.

To my best friend of twenty-eight years, Errol Cameron (gone but never forgotten), who taught me the true meaning of friendship; and to my ancestors (grandparents, great-grandparents, etc.) who have each left a little piece of themselves within me.

Linford Sweeney

Preface

Many years ago, I was privileged to hear stories of struggle, dreams, hopes and freedom from older family members and their friends.

My first recollection of these stories came from my father when I was three years old. Although impatient and semi-literate, he would read Biblical stories to me from an old Bible that included many drawings and paintings. When he left for England that book fuelled my fertile imagination, together with other stories from my grandparents - Elvy Bryan, Eliza Craig and Alexander Spencer. Within a five-year period between the ages of three and eight I was exposed to the richness and struggles of Jamaica's immediate past.

I entered elementary school at four years old, where I began the process of learning to read and write. I was considered a 'bright' child because I asked lots of questions and enjoyed reading. Several years later I left Jamaica with my mother to join my father in England. It was here that I heard more Jamaican amusing stories from my father and his friends as they regularly gathered in our house to play dominoes on a Saturday night. There were many stories about life in Jamaica over the past one hundred or so years – the struggles, the good times, ghost and "tall stories", and their many hopes and dreams that had only partially been realised or not been realised at all.

Dreams of Freedom

My greatest inspiration came from my mother, Rettynellar, who instilled in me the life-long desire to want to know more about my family and their past. My insistence on asking questions revealed quite a colourful and vibrant past that led me to find out even more about my family's history.

Around twenty-six years ago I became interested in researching my family history and discovered that my great-grandfather three times removed had arrived on a slave ship from Africa! Twelve years ago I decided to share my interest in my family's past, and Jamaica's history, with others. I went on to deliver classes and workshops to people who wanted to trace their family history and know more about their Caribbean past.

Today, I continue to research my family's history, educate others about their vibrant historical past, and carry out research into the culture and heritage of Caribbean communities. However, more importantly, I also write about my favourite subject – the history of Africa and its many descendants throughout the world.

Stories of Resistance and Emancipation

Voices of the Ancestors

There was no breeze blowing in the mass of trees surrounding the area where the once mighty Ashanti warrior had taken refuge from the chasing pack of hounds. It was a dark and peaceful night, as most nights were meant to be, except for a faint light from the overhanging full moon. Cudjoe, as he was known to his family, and John to the master and other workers, strained his ears to listen for the pursuing footsteps of the mob of killers that were calling for his blood. At first, he could hear nothing. And yet, true to his training, he remained still for a little while longer.

Suddenly he was startled by a sharp noise coming from the undergrowth. He felt a twinge of nervousness run up his spine, and his body reacted by quickly crouching so as to be closer to the ground and more able to pounce or run should the occasion arise. Cudjoe looked and widened his eyes to catch the little moonlight that he felt had come out to wish him a safe journey back to his people. He could see no movement as he quickly surveyed the area. His ears, once more, were alert to any further noises or movement around him but none came, and he put it down to a small animal making its way home. Cudjoe chose a tree and leant against its trunk so as to catch his breath before moving on towards his goal – to rejoin his people and the warriors that had gone before him.

In the silence, he had flashbacks to the last time he had run away from the plantation. For this, he had been severely lashed to within an inch of his life. The supervisor had been given the task of teaching him a lesson that he would never forget. Cudjoe never forgot that lesson. But it was not enough to stop him running away again. The desire to escape, and to be free, was stronger than the smell of death. It was something that the white men could never come to understand since they had never tasted the indignity of captivity. They had never sold to the highest bidder at an inhumane auction house where men and women were prodded, opened up and felt within the public gaze of others.

After the last flogging, the women on the estate had nursed his bloodstained and torn body back to health. He was so indebted to them. But they warned him about running away again. It was not worth it; they had all said.

One woman told him: "No go duh dat. Dey go kill yu dead."

He remembered cringing in pain each time they touched and tended to his body. He had listened to their concerned voices. Another woman kept on repeating those words and sounded so much like a squealing pig that was being chased around the pens to be slaughtered and roasted so as to satisfy the master's next meal. Even so, he had so much respect for each and every one of the women that had cared for him. However, although well-meaning, thought Cudjoe, none of them had any idea what it was like to be a man in captivity. Cudjoe knew only too well that the black man on a plantation was continually denuded of all his manhood, sense of responsibility for his family, and especially his children. Even his thoughts were controlled by a constant brainwashing that set brother against brother and father against son.

It was a case of divide and rule. The evillest ways that the white man brought with them to the plantation was to alienate a man from the women around him. They forced women, enslaved women, to prostitute themselves for the cause and pleasure of the white men - who had fewer white females around them. It seemed to suit them to have their way with black women whom they would in one breath call half human and in the other breath creatures to be physically desired.

Since arriving at the Dawkins plantation, Cudjoe had experienced humiliation after humiliation meted out by the master and his henchmen. And he knew that if he were caught again, it would be the end of his short life. So it was now or never. He had to be more careful than he had ever been before. Earlier, he had heard the dogs barking in the distance, but he had covered his tracks well. He was living in a land of many rivers, and it was easy for dogs to lose the scent of a careful and smart runaway. In a previous escape attempt, Cudjoe had lost his direction and had circled back toward the plantation since he was not familiar with the layout of the land. On the second occasion, he had run as far as he could only to be followed and caught by several other slaves who had been trained to retrieve runaways. This time, Cudjoe had taken care of the layout issue and the 'traitors' who had caught him the last time.

Cudjoe had now rested enough to continue his journey. Again he listened for any unusual noises and watched for sudden movements between the trees and within the undergrowth. He heard and saw nothing. However, he decided to be doubly sure and waited a while longer. Eventually, he moved away from a tree on which he had been leaning and slowly and softly picked his way along an unusually well-trodden path and continued to do this for about a further mile or so until he once again rested. This time,

Dreams of Freedom

Cudjoe found himself underneath a large tree and so he sat down for awhile to listen for unusual noises. As he listened, he was entertained by an orchestra of insects that played their harmonies, rhythms and melodies as sweetly as the voices and drums in the villages of his motherland.

With such beautiful sounds, he was tempted to fall asleep but thought better of it. And yet his mind kept on taking him back to the time when his mother would gently rock him to sleep as she would continue to carry out the household chores. He remembered her beautiful big brown eyes and her infectious laughter that always brought a smile to his father's face. Cudjoe always kept the memories of his mother and father with him wherever he went. He knew that their memories kept him sane and brave when all around him others would fall into the demonic world that had so cruelly devoured their freedom.

It was then that he heard the faint barking of dogs. He quickly rose from his royal seat donated by the forest orchestra and stood militaristic to attention. Based on his reckoning it was several more miles before he would reach the next river and so he made up his mind to leave at once. He could hear the barking dogs getting closer and so he decided to move a little faster.

Back home in Africa, Cudjoe had lived on open grasslands with his family and fellow villagers and sometimes ventured into the larger towns. There was little need to enter the forests unless for special hunts. However, he had been taught to move swiftly through forested and bushy areas like the leopards of the night had done in his homeland. Cudjoe decided to emulate the fabled creatures, and soon he could hear no barking dogs behind him. He continued moving swiftly through the darkness and ensuring that his feet would not be entangled in the undergrowth. He was taking no chances this time as the black hunters who had been trained to capture and return runaways had caught him unawares last time. Then he had stopped after believing that the dogs and their white ghostly handlers were no longer following, only to be surrounded and shackled once more much like a vicious wild animal.

Cudjoe had long known that the humiliation, when caught, was only less painful than the disappointment of not joining his people high up in the hills where freedom looked down on the fallen and fettered. Since then, every night he dreamt of being with his brothers and sisters in the faraway place that continued to call his name. Each night he visualised the celebrations that would be held on his return to the fold in the motherland.

In the place of his birth, the land of his ancestors, where he had grown to be a man, Cudjoe had ventured into the forests on some occasions and was able, after much training, to melt into the night like the fabled creatures he had heard about. On one occasion he had seen one such creature and watched it as it also watched him watch it pass by closely. He was on a great hill at the time – sitting in a tree with several other young warriors.

The trek to the areas that the beasts inhabited was part of his rites of passage to manhood, and he had only that same day attained that position. Even though the new land far from his motherland was different, there were some similarities and the sounds that he could hear were not too different to what he had heard back then. His father, the wise warrior chief of his village, had taught him combat and survival. In his land, during the war, the enemy always attacked by stealth, and so his training in such techniques and strategies were thorough and complete. Cudjoe had been groomed to become a future leader of his people.

As he made his way through the forest, Cudjoe felt a sickness deep within his stomach. It was something akin to a longing for home. He was once again stirred by thoughts of freedom, dignity and the principles and values of his people that he still held closely to his chest. In the new land, those ways were not respected. Cudjoe could not understand for what honour the white man lived or fought. They had no mercy for the dignity of those enslaved, and they continued to humiliate, maim and kill anyone that dared to oppose them. White men were filled with pride since they claimed ownership of land, animals and the people that they enslaved. Cudjoe's mind was filled with so much hatred for the white man as he stealthily and determinedly made his way to the river. And yet he knew that, along with the hatred, there was also mercy and a dignity powerful enough to forgive. However, it would take all that he had learned from the ancestors and his father to forgive. Neither would he ever forget.

As he continued on his relentless journey, Cudjoe remembered to thank his ancestors for their continued protection and support before he slowly moved into a large clearing within the trees. He also realised that a slow pace across such a vast open space would be useless, and so he decided to run. He made his way to the edge of the clearing and stopped. He looked around, listened and, without further hesitation, quickly ran across until he was on the other side, where he once again melted into the forest.

In his land, the ancestors, as warriors setting out to battle, would invite courage through dances, songs, food, healing potions and many other gifts bestowed before they were sent on their way.

Cudjoe asked for the gift of stealth and cunning and to be anointed from head to toe with their courage and determination. In his head, he was singing a warrior's song and hearing the rhythmic beat of the talking drums that sent news of his coming victory.

By that time Cudjoe's eyes had grown accustomed to the darkness, and his way seemed much clearer as he continued his journey home. In a dim and uncertain moonlight there appeared to his eyes what looked like a mirage in the night. And he could just about make out several shadowy figures going on before him. That stopped him in his tracks, and a tingle of fear dashed down his spine, setting off a myriad of emotions throughout his aching and tired body. The first thought that came to mind was that his pursuers had once again found him wanting. However, Cudjoe reached out for his ancestors, the rhythms, the dances, the songs, and quickly dismissed his enemies from his mind. They would not go before him surmised Cudjoe. He concluded that his ancestors were showing him the way ahead. They were there and ready to protect him on the most perilous and fearful part of the journey. His heart said follow; and he followed, knowing where he had to go. He saw the road ahead, and each step pushed him onwards to his final destination.

Cudjoe had to join the others that had gone before. For a long time, he had known about the many runaways from his, and several other neighbouring plantations, that had made it to the hills and freedom beyond. There were also many unseen paths, unknown to the white planters and their allies that led to the rocky, hilly and mountainous regions within the interior of the island. The ancestors had disguised the routes so that the white man could not follow. That place in the hills beyond, it had been said, stood close to the clouds and from there they could almost see the faces of the ancestors.

To reach that glorious place Cudjoe had to move as stealthily and silently as a black panther stalking its prey within the heart of the savannas of his homeland. Suddenly, as he came upon yet another clearing in the forest, he heard the sound of footsteps. He stopped and listened carefully. There were no dogs barking, no voices to hear, and the footsteps were faint. And yet he heard each footstep as they came towards him. He knelt down by a large tree for awhile to assess the situation and contemplate potential fight or flight strategies. Were they friend or foe? Could the ancestors have been wrong to lead him in the direction of which he had arrived? Cudjoe put negative thoughts out of his mind and concentrated on what his senses were trying to tell him. Once again, his pulse began to race, and he was ready to handle the situation – whatever it had planned for him. There was no going back this time. He knew that this was his last chance to live. To be captured would invariably mean death at the hands of his captors.

At that crucial point, when death presented itself in his mind, Cudjoe's thoughts turned to his family and whether he would ever see them again. His mind took him back to when his father had taught him to read the signs that spirits and the ancestors had passed on. He was to allow the spirits to surround him during times of indecision or threat and to fill his head with their collective wisdom. Silently, Cudjoe called on the spirits and slowly raised his hands to the heavens. In his mind and heart he was thinking: release me, unchain me, set me free.

Suddenly, before he could complete his prayer, Cudjoe heard a sound behind him, and quickly stopped and turned around. It was the faint voice of a man. He searched the darkness but could see nobody. He heard the voice again. There was a change in its faintness or tone. He was careful not to disturb the bushes or twigs around him. Neither did he utter a word or even dared to breathe. The voice spoke once more. This time, he heard the words clearly: "You are safe from harm". Was this the voice of the ancestors, thought Cudjoe? He also wondered whether it was a trick to lure him into a false sense of security. And yet, the voice spoke in his native language. Cudjoe knew that nobody on the plantation spoke his language or even his dialect. He heard his dialect, Twi, spoken in a soothing voice – much like his father would speak to him. He relaxed a little and inhaled deeply.

The voice spoke once more. This time, on hearing the word 'safe', Cudjoe breathed slowly and inhaled the life-giving air that surrounded him. However, Cudjoe, being a cautious man and a fierce warrior, kept himself hidden. He remained alert to any sudden movement or attack for a little while longer. His thoughts were of defiance. He had come too far to turn back; he was never to return to that cesspit of a place, namely the plantation. He was determined to regain the freedom cruelly taken away by his captors during a time of war between his people and the white man with his treacherous ways. A time when he was ripped from his people's arms, enchained, forced to march to the shores of the great ocean, before being packed on a ship that sailed many moons before land was sighted.

Cudjoe remembered the plight of those who did not make it during the gruelling and weary march to the shore. He recalled others who had not survived the long sea voyage to the new land as they were thrown overboard like cargo, and following sharks ate their flesh. And the arrival in the new land where they were auctioned to the highest bidder and forced to work day and night to fill the pockets of white men that had travelled from their lands far away across the vast ocean. These were the thoughts running through Cudjoe's mind. There was no other choice.

Cudjoe stood up and stretched his lean, muscular and scarred frame like the warrior that he was so as to face whatsoever had surrounded him. In his hand was a large stick that he had found on the ground where he had waited. His muscles tensed, and he felt the energies, courage and wisdom of the ancestors flowing through his very being – the blood of the warrior, defiant and aching to be free. He called upon the courage of his father a great and successful warrior to witness the strength of his son in battle. He also called for the determination and resilience of the lioness that stalked and fell its prey during the hunt. Again, Cudjoe wondered whether he had been discovered by friend or foe. A friend would be gentle, tactful and reassuring. The enemy would strike without warning.

The faint voice heard earlier was closer and clearer. The same words as before were repeated in a quiet and gentle voice. Then a reassuring hand was felt on Cudjoe's right shoulder; that gave him the answer.

Dilemma

Johnny did not have the courage to tell him the truth. It would have killed Kwaku if he knew what had happened. In fact, the secret went to the heart of Maroon community life in the islands thought Johnny. If it were to be revealed, then many people would be adversely affected. Johnny knew the secret but dared to tell anyone until an appointed time which was yet to be decided. He felt like judge and executioner and wanted to be sick at the mere thought of it. He realised that the terrible burden was too much for one man to carry and something had to be done before it was too late.

Even Johnny, a man of his word, was heavy with the tremendous guilt. He reflected on the whole sorry affair, and his confused mind switched between past and present. He sat in his favoured place, on a hill – known as Lookout Point – where villagers could survey as far as the eye could see. The village was hidden well and sat handsomely behind him. He agonised and contemplated what he should do.

His wife had once said to him, "Johnny you are a man of honour and truth, and you have no bad bone in your body."

It was good to know that his wife could identify his best qualities so well and yet it felt like a rope around his neck. And as every option spun around in his battered and sore head he managed to raise his eyes to see the sun as it rose in a beautiful haze from the east.

"I wonder what cruelty fate may have in store for the village today?" he asked himself, without needing to know the answer.

The hill where Johnny sat was used as a place from which to spot plantation-sponsored raiding parties led by Mosquito Indians who had agreed to lead the white militia to their hideaway. The last raid, as with all the others, was unsuccessful, and many soldiers were killed. The day that they became successful would be a day of shame and moaning for all the villagers since they had come to love their freedom once more. To Johnny, his past life on the sugar plantation was now just a distant and painful memory. It had been like living in a place of demons, and he was so glad to be free to enjoy his life in the village. He and his family were now thriving as they went about their daily lives. This secret was likely to change all that he had come to cherish. In his head, no real solution stood tall and with courage could be pointed out to the village elders.

It had not seemed fair to tell anyone else and so Johnny would stay awake all night and pondered over the trickiness of the situation. In his original village far away across the ocean, the people always consulted the elders about such matters. It was then debated openly and sometimes with major differences of opinion before the chief would make a decision on the matter. Johnny remembered once when a man had stolen from a relative, and he was eventually caught in possession of the stolen items. That same day the elders brought him into the village square – with the stolen properties – and called the village dwellers together for the hearing.
His relatives were given pride of place next to the elders, and each examined that which had been stolen and duly acknowledged the possessions to be their own. The elders proceeded to question the thief and in so doing, and after some quite brutal questioning,

found him guilty. The punishment was severe since that was not the first time the man had stolen. In fact, many other items were found in his possession, and the owners were reunited with their properties. Ultimately, the thief was flogged severely and then taken to the village boundaries, thrown to the ground and told never to show his face in the village ever again.

Johnny wondered whether he should ask the village elders about what to do. After all, it was in keeping with the time-honoured traditions practised by his people and many others like them. Or maybe, he thought, he could make his way down to the plantation to find out for himself. However, he realised that his going would have been a risky move and that if he were caught it would mean instant death. Whatever decision he would come to he knew that that was going to be a tricky one to explain to a man who had already dedicated himself to bringing freedom to many and helping to build a structured and peaceful village life. There were great honour and pride in the man's face, and that could be seen in the way he walked each day through the village.

That same day, after all, his chores had finished, Johnny made a brave but fully considered decision. He would speak privately with one of the elders. It was not his first choice in the beginning since the very matter was both complex and personal. However, he had come to realise that the secret was resting much too heavy on his shoulders, and people had a right to know the truth. Speaking to one elder was not the way things were done in the village, and the whole thing could backfire on him. But Johnny knew that sometimes a private word with another could cool down a volatile situation.

If anyone could have understood his predicament, Johnny thought, it would be that man. He had approached him in the past on several very delicate matters and was certain in his mind that the elder would fully understand his dilemma and act accordingly and with tact. The man was a godsend when he first escaped to the village. He had greeted him with open arms, and strongly supported Johnny's raid on the plantation when he had decided to rescue his wife and children.

The man was one of his closest confidantes and Johnny was glad that he could consult him about anything, and he was always likely to receive a fair and instant response. However, this was not one of those times. As Johnny greeted Kwesi, the elder he had come to know so well, and they smiled and exchanged pleasantries, he felt a sinking feeling in his stomach. "Is this a good idea?" thought Johnny as he continued to wrestle with whether or not he had made the right decision. "Maybe," he reassured himself, "it won't be so bad." Then he unfolded the story of his dilemma to the elder. Kwesi listened for a time, but Johnny noticed that he was becoming more and more agitated as he continued to tell the story.

What Johnny noticed about the elder on that occasion was that he asked so many accusing questions. Nevertheless, although feeling a little nervous about the possible outcome, Johnny continued. In his mind, he was thinking: "Was it a wise move to speak of such matters to the elder?". Johnny was by that time feeling a sense of betrayal coming from the elder. However, it was too late by then. All of a sudden Kwesi threw up his hands into the air, stood up and began to shout in such a way that Johnny knew that his gut feelings had been correct.

In village life, where there were many arguments and disagreements, it was customary that others would be summoned by a raised voice or raised voices. It was a cue for others to 'come running', become involved in the contention and to get to know the ins and outs of another person's private life. Some would say that there is no such thing as privacy in a village.

On many occasions raised voices was a way to sound the alarm whenever wrong was being perpetrated against an individual or group within the village. Johnny was keen to keep the discussion between the two men but realised that this was not to be. Others came to find out what the commotion was all about. Johnny was nervous and did not wait to explain but rose from his seat and, before he could be asked any further questions, ran into the nearby bushes. In his humble opinion, Johnny knew how serious the situation had become. He had a major dilemma.

It was midday the following day before Johnny ventured out of his makeshift hideaway in the overgrown bushes a little way from the village. He was tired since he had spent the whole night wondering about the dilemma he had come up against and the cowardice way in which he had left the company of Kwesi and the gathering throng. He realised that Kwesi was undoubtedly unhappy with the contents of his story. Johnny wondered whether he could have approached it differently but felt that he had had no other option. "Maybe I should have mentioned names," he thought. He deliberated with himself long and hard before concluding that the situation had already gotten out of hand, and it was something only he could fix.

Johnny was now sure that all the villagers had become aware of what took place with Kwesi the day before. His family would be worried about him and wondering what had been going on. He was torn between loyalty to his family and loyalty to the village. In truth, he had already come to the conclusion that the village, and the freedom that it gave to so many, was much more important than one family - or even one person. There were now many families living together in harmony and enjoying their new and more humane life in the hills. Johnny recognised that, as his wife had said, he was a truthful and honourable man. He, therefore, accepted that the time had come to make the story known to everyone.

Johnny realised that his courage had deserted him when he had needed it most. To run away like a frightened animal and looking like a guilty man in flight was not a good sign. It was said that one day he too may become chief of the village and therefore his behaviour had to be exemplary. And the bush was no place to be at night. It was much better than staying in the village, he thought. He considered his next move.

It was evening, and the sun had vacated the sky so that the moon could take over to commune with nature for a time - much like an elder ready to listen, thought Johnny. As he continued to look into the sky, he noticed that the stars were also looking down and seemed as spectators in a crowd gathered to witness the outcome of the story. He wondered where courage was made and whether he could find it before his whole reputation was tarnished forever.

Johnny spent the afternoon planning his strategy; one designed to reveal the full story and to save the village from what he considered being imminent destruction ahead. There was no longer any time available to think about any other outcome. "It was now or never", he thought as he felt an inkling of courage rising from within his embattled body. He could hear the ancestors and their wise words circulating in his mind. That was all that he needed to make his next move.

Johnny left his very well-concealed hiding place, tentatively picked his way through the forest of trees and bushes and entered the clearing leading into the centre of the village. However, before he could reach the gathering place, someone in the shadows caught his attention. He recognised the person. It was his wife who beckoned him from behind the storehouse. It seemed as if she had been waiting for him to return. She expressed her grave concern for his safety and did so in a quiet whisper. Johnny responded and made it clear that everything was going to be alright.

"A will come back," said Johnny as he touched his wife's hand before turning and melting into the darkness once more.

On a cool night filled with a myriad of radiant and glittering stars, Johnny had regained his courage. He always knew deep down that the son of a chief had no cause to fear anyone. He remembered his father's last words to him before the raid on their village: "Fear captures hearts and minds, courage brings freedom." Johnny had an important responsibility to his warriors and the dignity that was caught in his stance. He portrayed it all in his slow but powerful walk to the village square.

On being recognised, he was immediately seized by several lookouts that had been placed in strategic positions to watch out for enemy action - and for Johnny's return. The men were asked by Johnny to unhand him or face the consequences. They obeyed and asked where he was going. After stating his destination, the men accompanied Johnny to gather the elders. He called for the elders to join him in the village square.

In their own time, the chief and each of the elders appeared one by one from their respective dwellings carrying sombre and grave looks upon their faces. They were silent as they sat down and seemed ready to hear Johnny's explanation as to his uncharacteristic behaviour. However, before Johnny could begin, the elders asked for silence. The chief spoke first. He had waited for the villagers to gather together in the square and then he quickly recounted the earlier episode leading up to the meeting. After everyone had been updated, Johnny was brought closer to the elders and in full view of all the villagers.

Johnny, standing before the elders, looked around to survey the confused faces of elders and villagers that had surrounded him. In the crowd, he also saw his wife and children and his brothers, Accompong and Kofi. He took a long, hard look at Kofi, his youngest brother, before addressing the villagers. He then spoke to the onlookers. He took his time and began by refreshing everyone's minds about what had led up to the current meeting. He did not go into any details but continued with a history lesson. Johnny's knowledge of the journey taken by his forefathers was second to none in the village, and all listened in silence.

"I always bring your mind to think about the ancestors," Said Johnny, "our ancestors."

He reminded villagers of African times - before captivity - and the freedom and security that had once belonged to the ancestors. The more senior members of the village, men and women, shook their heads in acknowledgement. The village elders listened intently to

Johnny's story. He then gave a vivid account of their capture, being held in the dungeons, shipped across the sea in great numbers and enslaved on landing in a foreign land. Johnny's eyes were filled with both rage and longing as he continued his story. The emotion was too much for some as they wiped away their tears.

Johnny addressed the demonic plantation system that daily maimed and killed his people and allowed many others to be brainwashed into spying on their sisters and brothers.

"Spying for the white man is despicable because people die," stated Johnny.

There were uneasy movements among several people at the gathering.

"Accepting runaways was both honourable and dangerous", stated Johnny.

Johnny's final words about the origins of the villagers were to commend those who had found the courage to run away from the brutality meted out to men, women and children. He praised the courage, skills and determination of others to remain free in villages like the one to which he belonged. The elders and villagers all welcomed Johnny's story and gave their approval in cheers, positive comments and sporadic outbursts of song and dance.

"I been carrying a heavy burden," said Johnny "since I found out something a few days ago that made me incredibly sad."

Johnny took a deep breath before continuing. There was a tear in his eye too.

"I found out we have a spy in the village," said Johnny.

As he said it the mouths of the elders and the villagers opened wide with disbelief. Some people were eyeing up their neighbour as if to say "Is you the spy?" Many made it clear that they could never be the spy. One villager called Johnny a liar and stormed off, only to return a few seconds later to face Johnny once more.

The chief rose up to calm the throng. After the voices had all died down, and the elders regained order, Johnny looked in the direction of his family with sadness in his eyes. He saw his wife and children, his sisters and two brothers. Johnny's eyes focused on his eldest brother Kwaku. There were gasps from people. As Johnny turned from Kwaku's face, his gaze fell upon Kofi, his and Kwaku's beloved younger brother. Kofi seemed afraid, and Johnny knew why.

"As you all know, freedom comes first - even before family," stated Johnny.
Johnny then slowly pointed to Kofi, his younger brother.

"My beloved younger brother is the spy," shouted Johnny.

Kofi was someone that the plantation masters had recruited to infiltrate and destroy the village and return all free men, women and child to slavery. He was the demon spoken of by many who feared a return to the indignity and cruelty of plantation life. ·These people were spoken of but never seen. However, his time had come, and the finger of shame had been pointed his way.

"He my brother who bring shame on all in this place. He my brother, I love him, but know him not", said Johnny in a shaky voice that eventually cracked under the strain he had been through.

He broke down and cried. Kofi was seized.

Horse Tales

John was extremely excited on that day. So much so that he jumped on to the cart and failed to find the correct place to sit; slipping, falling and landing awkwardly on his behind. He quickly got up, embarrassed, and yet beaming from ear to ear for Master George to see. And all around him, there had been laughter.

"You drop on you behind like say ground turn mud," noted one laughing onlooker as they all stood by to watch John leave. He quickly found the space on the back of the cart just before Master George put the horses into motion. The small cart was laden with goods grown on the plantation and soon to be exchanged for much-needed products to be used in the Big House.

John had never been to the big town before and considered it to be a privilege to accompany Master George on that occasion. As he was leaving the plantation, John remembered that he was careful to ensure that everyone who had ears knew that he was going to the town.

"Me gone a town" John remembered saying, "a riding with Master George."

He had danced and sang his heart out, and everyone watched and realised that he had stepped up from being a mere field hand to being a stable boy before rising to the lofty heights of cart boy for Master George. As John made his way into town with Master John, he wondered when he would get the chance to take the reins himself. On this occasion, the Master had insisted on going alone into town. John thought about that, and it quickly came to his mind that there were rumours he had another woman living there. John then realised that Master George was a sly man. John was excitedly looking around, grinning from ear to ear and taking in the massiveness of the town as they drew near.

John passed other slaves walking by, and he smiled proudly and straightened up himself on the back of the cart. Along the way into the town he had to shift his position from one buttock to the other as the wooden seat he had been sitting on for almost an hour was hard and the road was rough and unforgiving. Master George had a cushion made from straw that he sat on, and which made his journey much more comfortable than John's own as they silently continued into the town.

"You will unload all the goods, take the horses to the farrier and load up before we leave," commanded Master George in a loud and deliberate way so that every passerby could hear.

"Yes, Master George, Yes sir," replied John in an almost inaudible voice.

"You heard what I said, boy?" asked Master George.

And before John could say a word Master George repeated what he had already told him.

"Yes, Master George, Yes sir," replied John once more, but this time in a louder voice.

John got to thinking and wondered whether the master had him for a fool. He already knew the ways of the white men, and deep down he craved his freedom.

In the town the road was smooth, and John felt a great comfort running through his body as he entered what seemed like the main square since there was much activity going on. Obviously, he was very glad to reach and quite soon Master George directed the horses towards a large store at the very centre of the main square. As John alighted from the cart, holding his sore behind with one hand and running around to the front to keep the horses steady with the other, Master George directed him to secure the animals and then to carry the goods from the cart into the store. John wondered why all white people spoke to black people as if they were idiots since Master George had told him twice what he had to do. He tied the horses to a post as he was ordered and carried the goods into the store closely watched by Master George, who by that time was stood surveying the streets and watching several young white women as they passed by. John dared not look at the women since it was an action punishable by a severe lashing or even death. However, he caught glimpses of Master George smiling with the women as they too flirted with him.

It was always a tricky thing to do, considered John – for black people to watch white people without them knowing that they were being watched. However, it was part of the black man's survival technique and everyone had to learn how to do it well. Although he struggled to carry several items John knew better than to complain or even, god forbid, drop anything. At one point as he was returning for what seemed like the tenth time from the store John wondered about Master George. "Would it be too much to help me with the heavy load?" he thought to himself. At that time

Dreams of Freedom

Master George was leaning nonchalantly against a post and watching John as he went back and forth.

John quickly dismissed the thought which, if known, would have resulted in some punishment when they got back to the plantation - or even out in the town's square. John realised that white men were vain, proud and egotistical and would rather show their brutality than to lose face. So he continued to struggle with each load, and in his way, he made each trip look more comfortable than it was. Finally, he completed the task. It was back-breaking work, but he considered himself the man for the job, and anyway accompanying Master George into the big town was his reward.

There was much that he could learn in the big town because he had his eyes on freedom one day. Immediately after completing one task he was then directed to where the horses could drink, be rubbed down and have their feet tended to.

John obediently untied the horses and went, where he was directed, a little distance down the street, to carry out his next duty. However, he was very thirsty and wondered where he could get himself a drink in the town. Slaves were never allowed in any place where white people stayed or visited unless they were house slaves waiting on the occupants. Therefore, water was not easily come by for slaves that were thirsty. Some masters would bring water barrels for slaves from which they could drink. In his haste to come into town to watch the pretty girls, his master had forgotten to bring such an important item. However, this understanding was something that was important to the slave, not the master.

John eventually arrived at the farrier's yard, with money given to him by the master, and allowed the horses to drink before their rub down and to have their shoes checked. John kept on looking toward the water trough as a man came out of the workshop and watched him. The man beckoned John to drink from the trough too. The figure standing there was an enormous black man with arms the size of sledgehammers. John was young, small with arms as thin as twigs. He decided not to argue with the man and quickly lowered himself to drink from the trough. When John had drunk his fill and wiped away the excess water from his mouth, he noticed the sneer on the other man's face. He then turned his back toward John and attended to the horses. John watched him work and wondered what kind of slave would be left alone to work with animals. John could see no white man around the farrier's yard. The man never said a word to John. Instead, when he had turned around, he regularly raised his head to watch John as he worked.

Since John was a child he had always been very inquisitive and nothing had changed as he grew into a youth.

"Mama, why those people so white? They look sick," John had blurted out on one occasion.

Many times John's desire to learn had gotten him into trouble with people on the plantation – from black, mulatto and white men. The plantation master was quite strict and oppressive with his punishments and never allowed slaves to get above their station. None could be taught to read or write since there were nothing more whites feared than the slaves rebelling against them - and literate slaves at that!

The slave population had grown tremendously over the years and the ratio, according to some, was now two hundred slaves for every white man on the island. John had noticed that there were fewer and fewer white people on the plantation and that several attempts at revolt had occurred. However, each conspiracy had been exposed by slaves loyal to the white men. John could never understand why slaves who were continually flogged or under the threat of being beaten or even killed would want to squeal on their friends and families. He had asked these questions of some slaves on the plantation, and this was quickly brought to the attention of the master. John remembered that he had been flogged several times because of his desire to learn. He was determined to keep from everyone, but his mother, that he could both read and write. He had been taught by an old woman who had in turn been taught by a white lady.

The man continued to watch John as he worked on the horses and sometimes stopped to look him straight in the eyes. John, who was not at all shaken by his strange behaviour, merely observed the man at work. Then the man suddenly stood to his full height and addressed John in a deep and gravel-like voice. "What you have on you mind?"

John did not have a ready answer and was taken aback by such a question. Even if he had had an answer, he knew that it was not a good thing to respond too quickly to questions. He had learned the hard way that thinking was not always a good thing in such circumstances. The man could be a spy, thought John. So he gathered his thoughts and uttered what was on his mind. He had no reason not to ask the question. "You is a slave like me?"

The man looked at John and considered his response for a moment as if trying to fathom John's true intentions for asking the question. John, as only he could be, was being inquisitive and knew that his question was an important one; although he knew not why. John was careful not to speak too loudly as informers were everywhere and they would run to the masters with any small thing that may be said between slaves. And in most cases, these people never fully understood what people were talking about before they decided to carry tales.

The man laughed quietly, came closer to John and told him something he was not expecting.

"I am no slave but a free man working my trade," he said. "I name Samuel. What you name?"

John had heard about black men who were free, but he had never met such a person - until that day. John wanted to know how he became a free man but dared not ask.

"Me name John," he answered.

Somehow, Samuel must have read his mind, and he told John all about his trade and how long he had been doing it. However, nothing was said that John could understand. The conversation was merely about the benefits of looking after the health of horses. At first, John did not understand what was being said as Samuel used a kind of coded language.
"This horse," and Samuel pointed to one of the horses "is very skilled at his job and been around many plantations. And he get watered and fed by good people."

John nodded.

"If the horse is a good worker you keep it and you give it freedom to roam," continued Samuel.

Dreams of Freedom

John was getting to understand the subtle codes that Samuel was using. He was transfixed to the spot for awhile as he listened to the storyteller as he weaved his magic and educated him about the proper care and treatment of horses.

Soon it was time to leave Samuel and return to loading up the cart with provisions for Master George. Samuel never looked at John as he left the yard but instead directed him to clear up the mess that the horses had made. It was not what John had hoped for at the end of such an eye-opening meeting. However, he obediently carried out his work filled with new energy and a great deal to look forward to. He handed Samuel the payment that he been given.

In the following years, John continued to learn about horses from everyone that he knew until one day he was rewarded for his efforts and purchased by a man only known as "The Farrier". John knew who had purchased him, and he was very thankful. Before long he earned his freedom and became a free man on the island of Jamaica.

Dreams of Freedom

Maryann came to see her mother one night to tell her that she was pregnant. She had been considering how she would tell her for the past few weeks when she had realised what was happening to her each morning. Her mother, like herself and everyone else, were up very early, and they also worked at opposite ends of the plantation. They saw one another at nightfall and were usually too tired to hold any real conversation before going to sleep. Maryann had seen many pregnancies in her time and knew what to look out for. But she was shocked that it happened to her. They were together just the once. However, she felt it was the right thing to do given the goings on around the plantation over the years.

After waiting for her mother to relax a little - and she was also getting a little sleepy too - Maryann decided that it was the right time to tell her.

However, at first, there was no courage standing by her side. That was something she needed at that time - more than anything else. Then courage came and took her hand.

"Mama," she said.

"Yes, child" replied her mother rather exhaustedly.

"I am pregnant". Maryann blurted it out as if another chance would not have passed her way again.

"What?" exclaimed her mother as she rose quickly from her bed in which she been resting to stare at her daughter with a shocked look on her face. She stood before Maryann with her hands akimbo.

She stood for a time just looking in amazement at her daughter before she sat down again on the bed and cried uncontrollably. Eventually, she wiped away her tears, pulled herself together and bravely rose from the creaking bed as if about the make some declaration. She then started to lecture Maryann about the situation.

"I always tell you no give master or his people them no cause to have them eyes on you", she snapped, "now look what you go do", she continued with even more tears in her eyes.

"But Mama...," Maryann tried to get her mother's attention, but she could not get the words out. And she would not allow her to while she was in full flow. Maryann knew that her mother, once fixed on talking about a subject, could not be budged. However, she thought, this time, it was different.

"Why they go trouble my one daughter, who me try to grow up good good?" She cried.

Maryann's mother was by now walking around the limited floor space in the one room house they shared, and each time she passed by her frock brushed against her daughter's face. Maryann shifted her position a little, but there was no more space to occupy in the room. Instead, she was considering what her mother had said about the master and the other white men on the plantation.

Although they believed her and her kind to be inferior and animal-like in looks and behaviour, none of the men found it unusual that they spent their time staring at and slobbering over all the young slave girls as they passed by. On many plantations, there were about eight white men to every white woman, and it was not surprising that they felt the need for company. It was not unknown for these girls to go unwillingly with men who were old enough to be their fathers or even grandfathers. In time, many became pregnant and gave birth to little mulatto children – where the mother is black, and the father is white. Maryann's mother and father always warned her and the other girls to keep away from the desperate white men.

"And another thing, they no have no shame", said Maryann's mother, "because they just take the young girl them in the bush and when they finish get what they want they just leave them and gone".

Maryann knew what her mother was talking about because it happened to her too. And she had a mulatto child to prove it. Then the master notice that the child was clever and took him from the family and sold him to another plantation many miles away. The master was always afraid that bright slaves would rise up, and the others would follow. He apparently believed that the boy got his intelligence from him and not from his black mother. Maryann's mother was silent for a while.

At that point, Maryann took her chance and said "It not for a white man, Mama".

She surprised herself at the courage she found to tell her mother she was getting it all wrong.

"You sure a noh white man child? You sure?" inquired her mother holding a look of disbelief on her wet face.

Maryann nodded that she was sure, and her mother's face broke out into a smile. She reached out and grabbed Maryann and kissed her on the forehead. Maryann watched as her mother danced around the room and in the process hit her knee against the bed. Immediately she sat down to rub the pain away, and while doing that her smile suddenly disappeared, and she looked carefully at her daughter.

"Then a who the child belong to then?" she quickly enquired.

Before Maryann could answer, her mother forgot about her aching knee, rose from the bed and began once again to lecture Maryann. The smile on her face had been replaced by a serious look of frustration verging on anger as she pointed her finger towards the door. Maryann knew what that meant and knew what was coming.

"A tell you a million time say you to stay away from the worthless boy them that we have around here. No true?"

Maryann nodded, but before she could say anything more the lecture became a tidal wave of attack on her person. It felt as if the ocean that had carried her grandparents to the land in which they inhabited had decided to swallow her and devoured her whole being.

"Noh tell me nothing. I noh want hear it!" her mother insisted.

She proceeded to become angrier as time went by, and her words, now more like a hurricane, just kept on coming and coming.

Maryann's mother went on to mention each boy by name, what they had done, where they did it and who they did it with. Each time there was a lull in the tirade, Maryann tried to explain, but her mother just looked at her as if to say "child, one more word and you taste my hand". Maryann's mother continued to flood her head with so much negativity, and gossip Maryann felt quite numb and helpless. So in the good traditional way she remembered that "a child should be seen and not heard" and simply sat on the side of the bed, kept quiet and listened for just a moment longer.

Her mother continued in an animated fashion, telling story after story, some from way back when she was a young girl and others in the last few years. Maryann felt as if she had gone into a deep sleep as she reflected that her mother was not old and still had what most men would admire in a good woman. Many men had tried to win her heart, and the same number had failed. To Maryann, it seemed as if her mother now considered herself an old maid. So, not for the first time, Maryann just drifted away into her well-rehearsed world of fantasy - into some kind of hypnotic state - as she watched her mother's movements and gestures and the gradual rise and fall of her voice, much like the melodies of a song. Maryann began to think about Joseph, the young man that she had admired so much for so long. In fact, if she had what the white man called a calendar, maybe she has had her eyes on him for the past two years or more. He was so gentle with her and so kind and had a lovely and forgiving nature. He always watched her as she passed by the stables on her way to the boiling house. Although Joseph was older than she was Maryann never noticed that and just fell deeply in love with the young man. She was so much in love with Joseph that she had no interest in anyone else on the plantation, and she always avoided the gaze of the white men whenever they passed by.

He was a stable boy, and he mingled with the white men and women on the plantation. Sometimes he would accompany the master when he went into the town. Joseph was always very polite to everybody and when he smiled he melted her heart. However, Maryann also knew that Joseph was no fool, and he was sure deep down that his freedom would come one day.

"Maryann", he would say when they eventually found time alone, "I pray every day for the time when we all become free".

Every time they met Joseph would openly share his dreams of freedom with her, and she had begun to share the same dreams too. She also recognised how important it was for Joseph's thoughts about the future to be kept secret. He always told her that the white men disliked slaves who thought about and planned for the future.

"Those niggers are dangerous and must be shown their place," Maryann once heard the master telling a visitor to the plantation.

"Joseph", she would tell him in a sweet and quiet voice, "you secret safe with me. A no going reveal it to no one".
So she took an oath with him never to reveal it to anyone else. Maryann thought how slaves were taught not to think since the white men feared more uprisings and rebellions from disgruntled slaves. Those who broke the rules were swiftly and cruelly dealt with, and their remains were sometimes left in full view of others. They hoped that such awful sights would serve as a deterrent to anyone else who harboured similar thoughts.

Maryann told Joseph "I so sad about so many people lose them life because they want freedom".

Dreams of Freedom

"The day will come when freedom will stop all the killing" replied Joseph.

For as long as it was possible they would both lay together in the moonlight, sometimes talking and sometimes cuddling up together, as they watched the stars entertain with their many twinkles.

Maryann was not sure how long she had been deep in thought, but she suddenly became aware that her mother had changed the topic of her lecture.

"What people going say when they know the state of me daughter?"

She almost whispered the words as if she feared that people were listening at the door.

"They going laugh at me" she said rather sadly.

Once more Maryann opened her mouth to speak, but her mother hushed her once more and dared her to open her mouth again. Maryann got the message loud and clear because she always had the utmost respect for her parents. And since the passing of her father from a severe and cruel beating last year she was all the more determined to look after her mother.

"Is what me a go do?" she lamented. "Maybe if a tell them…"

Maryann was drifting away once again. Life had been difficult for them both. Her mother had worked in the fields until the terrible accident that almost crippled her. She barely got out of the cane field with her life that day when a rebellious slave named Giant fought with the white men. As machetes were wielded, Maryann's mother had not moved out of the way in time, and her right foot was badly slashed by a machete. Maryann thought that her mother would die that day. But she valiantly fought for her life and survived. The doctor, a mullato man who had studied in England, did a wondrous work on her foot so that she could walk again.

"Mama, you going dead and leave me alone?" Maryann had said to her mother at the time. "You going leave just me one in this place?"

Maryann's mother had been in and out of a fever for several days before she became conscious once more.

On that occasion, she heard Maryann and said: "Hush child me going no way".

Luckily her foot was saved. But it was touch and go for awhile. And during all that time the plantation manager or the master never once came to see her. Her mother always told Maryann that that man was the worst manager the plantation had ever had.

Maryann suddenly returned to the room to hear her mother talking about Eliza's daughter who had gotten pregnant by one of the worthless boys.

"You know since she get pregnant a one embarrassment for her mother and the rest a family". Maryann knew the story and although she continued to watch her mother she decided not to listen anymore. Being quiet, she thought, was sometimes a good thing. It was a chance to reflect on things that had gone before.

Dreams of Freedom

She thought about her father and realised how she missed him so much now that things were hard for everyone. She particularly loved his words of comfort and the way he was so patient with her, and that he always called his baby. At this time, after her mother had gone through several of her many lectures, he would have taken her aside and tried to find out more about Joseph. His was a peaceful soul, and yet it was also a tortured soul given the conditions that he found himself in. But one thing was sure, she recalled that her father hated injustice.

Maryann realised how much of a gentleman her father had been - just like Joseph. Maryann, on first meeting Joseph, had commented to herself about Joseph: "This man remind me of Papa". She always told everyone that her father was a great man with strong principles about family. Just like Joseph, he had worked in the stables and sometimes he was allowed to look after the horses. He loved those horses and spent long hours talking to them about his troubles. The stables became a place where he could meditate upon life away from the many cruelties that existed around him. On one occasion, Maryann remembered, he said: "The horses never once complain about me laying me troubles at dem feet".

One day Maryann's father got it into his head that the horses were not being treated right by one of the manager's supervisors, a cantankerous white man named Henry, who always whipped the horses for no real reason at all. He never liked it too much, and he would say to him, in his very polite way, "Mister Henry the horse don't do nothing to you".

For that Henry would instead whip him for speaking out against him in that way. Then one day Henry decided to take the horsewhip to a young six-year-old black child who came to the stables to see the horses. As he whipped the child Maryann's father's blood begun to boil and he grabbed the whip from Henry's hand saying "That's enough now Mister Henry, he only a child, let his folks deal with him".

Maryann remembered a bystander telling her that Henry turned around, pulled out his knife and taunted her father. However, he was very strong and defended himself for a while before he had to strike Henry to avoid the stabbing that was surely coming to him. Henry fell, hit his head on a rock and died several days later from his injuries. Maryann remembered the commotion and people running into the fields to call her mother to tell her what was about to happen. He was taken to the punishment post, and without any questions asked, cruelly flogged to death. Everyone was devastated by this cruelty and injustice that occurred that day. But no one could say anything lest they too would befall the same fate. That was plantation justice. Maryann's mother never recovered from his death.

She vowed, "I'll never look on another man".

And she would sit and cry for many hours after darkness fell. Tears would also come to Maryann's eyes since she so respected and loved her father too.

Suddenly Maryann heard her mother calling her name. She looked up at her and stared into her eyes as if waiting for a beating.

"Maryann, you listening to what me say? She said. And moreover, why you crying and a no even lick you yet?"

Dreams of Freedom

Maryann had not realised that as she remembered her father and what had happened to him, and her mother's grief, tears had been coming to her eyes. Maryann knew that, although her mother was never heavy handed with her, she was not too big to be whipped, and she hurriedly wiped away the tears with the back of her hands. "A not crying Mama" she quickly announced.

It was then that her mother eventually decided to stop the lecture and talking about the business of everyone on the plantation but the master's dog. She sat down on the bed next to her daughter and looked at her with compassion in her eyes. Maryann knew how much her mother loved her, but she also knew, from what her father had told her, that "Love come different for different people". Her mother then asked the most important question that Maryann wanted to hear, and what she had been trying to tell her for so long.

"Who make you pregnant?" she asked.

It was not the most subtle of questions thought Maryann, but it was the right one. However, at first, she did not want to answer since she could not be sure whether her mother had stopped talking. Then she considered what she had wanted to say before her mother's lectures and anger had taken effect. "Do I have the courage to tell her?" she asked herself. Eventually, she plucked up the courage and started to tell her.

"He not a bad boy, Mama. He respectful like Papa was. A gentleman like him too. He love justice to, and he always treat me right." stated Maryann trying to soften her mother's heart before she told her.

"So what him call?" asked her mother, rushing her daughter and starting to smile again.

As her mother smiled, Maryann felt that she had the courage to answer her question. "He call Joseph" murmured Maryann under her breath.

"Tell me again make me hear good." said her mother.
"Joseph, Mama," said, Maryann.

This time, she said it a little louder so that her mother could hear much better. Sometimes her mother was very selective in her hearing, but most of the time she wanted people to speak louder so she can hear better.

"You mean Miss Liza Joseph? The one who at the stables and go a town with the white man them? And he have a nice smile just like Papa did?" said her mother excitedly.

"Yes, Mama," Maryann said rather coyly.

Maryann's mother cried out for mercy when she heard Joseph's name. She got up from the bed and ask Maryann the same question once more.

"A who you say the father is?

Maryann responded giving the same name and watched her mother as she rose from the bed and started to dance around the room, but taking care, this time, to avoid banging her leg against the table. Maryann never saw her mother dance like that before.

"So why you no tell me that before", she enquired, "and you make me go on so bad in the place".

Maryann knew her mother well and said nothing else. However, she was becoming a lot easier to talk to. This time, she allowed her to finish another series of questions that only her mother could ask. One such question surprised Maryann.

"So why you never bring him here before, I don't bite?"

When she noticed that her mother had stopped talking and was now in a better mood, Maryann smiled for the first time since she had told her the news about her pregnancy. She knew then that everything would be okay and that the future was going to be a better one. It was time for freedom to come to them all.

"We going to have a big wedding!" shouted her mother at the top of her voice as she made her way out of the door, knocking over the broom in her eagerness. Maryann could hear her mother calling Miss Eliza, and she just smiled and reminded herself that her family was going to be alright.

Several weeks later the news came that everyone was to be freed, and slavery had finally ended. Maryann only wished that her father could have been alive to see that day.

The Loyalty

Jacob was adamant that his youngest son, Isaac, would remain on the plantation.

For many years others had gone before, and many never had the chance to say goodbye. Those were sad times for all, and the intense pain quietly lingered for the lifetime of everyone concerned. In some strange way, it was always the strongest man or sturdiest women that were sold for the most money that the master could negotiate. In the past, many slaves attracted high rewards when sold or auctioned by their masters. However, it was widely known that, because of the hard times, that many slaves were now fetching little or nothing for the sellers. It seemed as if the plantations would be going through some tough times.

Jacob recognised that there was still hope for Isaac to remain with his family - where he belonged. It was his greatest wish to see him grow to be a man and be strong and handsome just like his father. And a free man at that! Jacob 's eldest son, Nathaniel, had been sold to another plantation that lies on the other side of the island. It had been like any other day when the master sent two men with guns and one of the black supervisors. They then proceeded to drag Nathaniel, just fourteen years old, kicking and screaming from the home he shared with his family. His mother, Sophie, could only look on as they escorted him up the dirt track to the waiting cart. Jacob saw it differently: it was market day, and the master had decided to choose his best cattle to be sold for handsome profits. Except that the cattle was human, and his eldest son.

Jacob had heard the screaming and tried to make his way from the cane field, but the supervisor had raised his gun and seemed serious about keeping him in the field. Nevertheless, Jacob still carried on running toward the house before a gunshot was heard and he felt the pain in his right leg. Jacob fell to the ground as his leg buckled beneath him. He also got a face full of dirt for his efforts. Later it was found that the bullet had entered and exited the calf muscles. That was a day he would never forget as long as he lived. They took his boy and as a father, he could not protect his son.

Jacob was once told that each slave belonged to the master. They were his property to do with whatever he wished. Jacob had enquired from the teller of the story about the children and whether they too were slaves. The story teller confirmed that all children born to slave mothers automatically became slaves from birth. It was then that he realised that parents had no rights over their own children - the ones that they brought into the world, cared for and loved. Like cattle, they could be taken away at any time. How must a man raise his son when someone else could take them away without your permission? Jacob asked himself. He would often wonder what happened to fathers who could not protect their children – a natural inclination. How do they take responsibility for their homes? How would those grieving mothers look at them and treat them? He already knew the answer to that question.

Jacob had seen so much injustice and bloodshed that with each passing day he grew tired of plantation life. However, he knew that he had something that many others did not have. He had something far greater. He had hope! Jacob had decided many years before that he would hitch his cart to a star and follow his dream. It was time to take responsibility for his family.

There had been many rumours going around that the plantations were to be abandoned since the British had hinted at abolishing slavery. How did Jacob know this? He would always tell others, with a wry smile, that a friend of a friend had told him. Many had learned, sometimes to their detriment, that knowing the names of these 'storytellers' was not always a wise thing. There had always been rumours and conspiracies whispered amongst the slaves, and as time went by care had to be taken with what was said. The eyes and ears of the plantation were many, and few knew where the next tale would surface, who would say it and because many slaves had been 'bought' by their masters, whether they would be friend or foe.

The temptation to "tell tales" on fellow slaves was always an interesting proposition, thought Jacob. A larger one bedroom house, a bigger garden or special treatment by the white men were all temptations for lowly and seemingly ambitious young field workers or house slaves. They never thought about the cruelty and injustice meted out to their families and friends. In fact, those people had no friends, and no one trusted them. They sometimes lived short lives, mostly filled with sadness and disappointment. That kind of precarious life was not for him, thought George.

Over time Jacob had heard a lot of talk about Africa from the old folks. The talk was mainly by women since most men used to die early through overwork. They would tell of long sea voyages from across 'the big river' and a land where people who looked like them lived freely - a place the white men called Africa. In this place, there were great kings and queens, mighty warriors, lush plantation, good food, and more importantly, freedom. Since he was a boy, he would listen intently and with great interest to the elders as they recounted stories upon stories. Soon, he found himself telling stories to children and adults alike. This had become a covert tradition on the plantation. Therefore, Jacob always grew his own identity based on the stories of the achievements of his ancestors.

Jacob had also heard rumours of an uprising on the plantation. He knew that it would not take long for it to happen and he readied himself to face whatever came his way. He wanted freedom but wanted to get it his own way and without bloodshed. However, he thought to himself, if he had to fight to defend his family he was prepared to do so. It was not too long before there were whispers, and much going to and fro for many slaves, before Jacob got his answer. There was a mob headed his way.

Jacob reached for his machete as the mob got closer and slowly ran his fingers down the blade with the precision of a true swordsman. He was always known for keeping a well-sharpened and impeccable tool. It was said that one blow from Jacob's machete took down many sugar cane plants in one mighty swing. It was never a good idea to mess with a 'swordsman' lest you lose your head. George was warrior material, sturdy and standing six feet five inches tall. It was said that he descended from Coromantee warriors who were forcibly brought to the islands two generations before. These warriors were fierce and fearless in battle.

As the mob grew ever closer, it was noticeable that they were slowing down, and they were probably thirty yards from Jacob's house, they had slowed to a simple shuffle. Men were looking at one another as if to say: 'Why wi doing dis?' Glances flew between them like bullets on a dysfunctional battlefield. Jacob called out to ask what they wanted, and none dared to reply. But then a thin and wiry young man came forward and apologetically asked for Jacob's support in overthrowing the master. George declined - and for good reason. It was found out later that the master had sent a slave boy to warn the local militia as he considered the gathering to be a rebellion.

The militia came the following day. The rebels had scattered, and some had left the plantation at nightfall the day before. They had been rumbled by a couple of informers from the mob. Others had stayed hoping that they would not be identified. They were pointed out by the informers and a severe punishment was meted out that day. The ringleaders were summarily executed. The militia made up of white and black men, then went in search of the runaways. The master called everyone together and gave a resolute and defiant speech outlining future punishment for any further attempts at rebellion. The rest of the day went by in silence.

Jacob was determined that Isaac would remain with the family. He was committed to seeing his son become a man. The kind of man that his father had become - proud, defiant and strong! And, as always, thoughts of his eldest son would also fill his head. During these times Jacob would find somewhere quiet to be with his thoughts. He wondered, as he did on each occasion, where his son would be, what he looked like and what he was doing. Jacob always considered searching for his son one day when freedom came. And he knew that the time was not far off for that dream to become a reality. It had been six years since he was taken and the time had come to unite his family once more. Jacob knew that as a man, he had to take responsibility for his family and set an example for his sons.

There was something in the air the next morning that few people could explain. Everyone woke up bright and early - which was the usual - and went happily to their work to harvest the canes that were now ready for market. The master had told everyone that he needed the money to keep the plantation operating and to ensure that they had food, clothing and shelter. Nobody wanted to be sold to bring in more money, and so by late afternoon they had completely harvested all the remaining plantation fields. The cane crusher had not seen a busier day.

It was in the coolness of the late afternoon that the master called everyone together and decided to make an announcement. Jacob already knew what was to be said because he had heard it from a friend of a friend. The announcement, but for a slight tremble in the master's voice, could have been any one of hundreds heard before. However, this time, the onlookers heard something they had never heard before. It was something that they would never hear again - or so they thought. The proclamation from the British King said, in a nutshell, that slavery had been abolished in all the Empire's territories. The whole place, comprising some three hundred slaves, was jubilant. To Jacob that meant freedom! And as he celebrated, his machete swung wildly until his wife asked him to put it away before he hurt somebody.

For Jacob, it was a last farewell to slavery and to man's inhumanity to man. However, the master had not finished his announcement and quickly asked for calm. The next few sentences became like a chain around everyone's neck - just like back in the days when the forefathers were captured and led involuntarily to the slave ships. The Master made it clear that only children up to the age of six would be truly free. People looked at one another with both disgust and amazement. The master concluded that everyone else would remain on the plantation as apprentices for five years. Then they would be set free. Jacob, for a while, raised his machete. As he looked around him, he felt the anger and frustration of every man, woman and child welled up inside.

Isaac and his mother stood and watched him with tears in their eyes. What could have been a celebration had turned into something more sombre. Isaac looked at his father, and something in his eyes melted his heart. After seeing the many guns pointed at the throng of what were effectively ex-slaves, Jacob lowered the machete. He still had his family to think about. As long as he was alive, he still had a dream to fulfil and hope in his heart.

An End to Pain

Gwen heard the commotion outside the small dwelling which she shared with twelve others, and quickly decided to go out to see what all the fuss was about.

"Is what going on over there?" asked Gwen looking in the direction of the small group of people that had formed in front of the big house.

There was no response from anyone but Aunt Dorothy whose words were not helpful in any way.

"A don't know mi-sef," she said, and sloped towards the commotion.

The day, as it had been for almost a week, was sunny and hot, and all had been quiet up until that point. The place that that Gwen shared and called home was a small building made of wood, standing on the ground on four posts, and having a zinc roof. There were just one room and a small veranda where a single guest could be welcomed - or even two at a push - and small wooden steps at the door leading down into the little yard space. To have a veranda, no matter how small, meant that Gwen had become quite an important person among the large slave community that inhabited the Williams Plantation.

The modest but sturdy house had been built by her late husband, William before he was cruelly taken from her a few months earlier. William had been an extraordinary man who learnt the art of house building when he had been a free man until unscrupulous white fortune hunters robbed him of his legitimate claim to freedom. His papers, given as part of the will of his former master, were destroyed, and he was duped into once more becoming a slave. In the end, he was flogged to death by the master's henchmen for protesting his innocence once too often. However, Gwen never had time to be a grieving widow as there was always work to be done and, as she would say about the master "compassion no did fine him when God was creating man."

Gwen shared her house, as do everyone else on the plantation, with other slaves. The majority were family members and their children, and the others were women who had lost their own partners or male family members.

Gwen was always heard to say "A woman should never be by herself". Few people, least of all Gwen, ever felt easy with so many people sharing one house, and relationships were sometimes at breaking point.

"Gwenie, people sleep bad in a this house. Me no sleep at all last night" was the usual mantra of one member of the household as she barely squeezed past Gwen on the veranda.

"A noh have nothing to say, I got a lot on me mind," Gwen retorted in a quiet voice. But inside she was thinking "Why she so ungrateful", but decided not to mention it to her.

"Somebody take way me apron" shouted another.

It was known that some people were 'thieves' and it was, therefore, important to know the people you talked to, Gwen would remind herself. She had no time for such people. Although known for keeping her own counsel, Gwen also knew when to speak up on behalf of those people who claimed to have been hard done by.

It was a hot Sunday morning, the temperature was still rising, and it was no time to be out in the scorching sun. However, Gwen knew that for six days a week all field slaves had to work in the hot sun without any real respite. She also knew that many had died needlessly due to what she heard the master call sunstroke.

"Miss Amy, you still a sleep?" was a lone voice in the midst of the commotion heard by Gwen.

"A tired Mother Joanna, and a can hardly walk" came the response from within another house.

On this particular morning, people were tending their small crops while others were just either catching up on sleep or tending to injuries and ailments. Many such injuries came from floggings received from the plantation's hired mercenaries, or they were wounds inflicted by supervisors, sometimes using machetes or even guns, on what they considered to be disobedient slaves. "Cruelty seem like dem middle name," Gwen would say to herself.
Although the master was against so many floggings and injuries, his concern was wholly selfish since he needed healthy workers in the fields. The master was no fool and showed this by ensuring that disobedient slaves were punished and used as examples for others to see.

"Morning Miss Gwen," said someone as they passed by.

"Morning Miss Claris. You look good today," replied Gwen, and continued to ponder life on the plantation. The cruelty meted out by humans to other humans was totally uncalled for thought Gwen. She had witnessed so many atrocities in her short life that it had started to become run-of-the-mill to her. Gwen realised that she was becoming desensitised to the horror that took place every day.

"You hear anything 'bout you son yet Miss Claris?" asked Gwen.

"No sah. Not a ting. It look like him gaan," the woman replied with sadness in her voice as she slowly shuffled away.

Gwen was aware that many years before a code was introduced stating that black people were three-fifths human, and that meant they could then be legitimately held as slaves, as property to anyone who had paid the price or bred from the same stock. The slave's owner also had the right to do whatever they wanted with 'their slaves', including selling, severely beating or even killing them. Nobody who was a slave had recourse to law or could be defended, and therefore slave owners were given complete authority over the lives of their slaves as both jury and executioner.

"No worry yourself Miss G, God will provide," said one woman to Gwen as she too passed on her way to tend her vegetable plot.

"Me know. Thank you," replied Gwen.

Gwen was a short woman who was in her thirties but who could have easily have been mistaken for fifty. Her life had been a hard one since, like many other slaves on plantations throughout the island, she had been put to work in the cane-fields as a young child.

Added to that fact was the complete and deliberate lack of reading and writing skills amongst plantation slaves.

As she thought about that Gwen smiled to herself. In fact, although some could read, teaching writing to slaves had been outlawed on all the islands. There was the case of one woman who worked in the big house, and she had been taught to read and write by the lady of the house. Many white women had nothing useful to do but wait for her man to return home each day and to look pretty when there was company at the big house. While the master was away, his wife occupied her time by teaching her maid how to read and write. Eventually, having learned quite quickly, this slave woman was able to help others become their eyes, and very soon all five hundred slaves on the plantation knew about her abilities. News of the woman's skills then reached the master's ears, and he was none too pleased, so much so that he promptly sold her to another plantation. Nothing had been heard of her since. This had been a harsh lesson to everyone on the plantation and Gwen was careful to ensure that all those who had such skills kept the knowledge a secret.

Gwen had her first child at the age of fourteen, and she continued to work the fields until the day she was ready to give birth. The following day, although in pain owing to a difficult delivery, she was back in the fields. This was life on the plantation even after slavery had been declared abolished.

Gwen came out of the house and into a small yard where she was allowed to plant selected crops so as to supplement the woeful income provided by the plantation. She was able to grow yam, dasheen, beans and peppers. Gwen found it hard to subsist on the meagre amounts that she and others were able to grow. The master ensured that the best crops on the most land were grown and sold for their own profit. To make it worst, the few pennies offered by the master for fourteen hours work each day was below her dignity. Sometimes she had to feed only the children, and the hunger pains were felt in the fields the following day. Working on an empty stomach was never easy and sometimes she collapsed in the heat. However, she recognised that it was the new system they called apprenticeships, which were introduced in eighteen thirty-four in the British colonies. The then King of England had ordered it to be so. Recently, Gwen and others had overheard that the King had died, and a woman was now Queen. If this was the case, thought Gwen, then she had to have more compassion since she was a woman.

When Gwen went outside, after hearing the commotion, she had noticed that people were gathered in front of the master's house. There were many raised voices coming from the direction of the big house, and many arguments could be heard. People wanted to know what was happening, and word came from within the big house. Apparently, some important news had been promised. Now Gwen already knew about the possibility of such a gathering but did not know when. You see, on plantations, there was no real system when dealing with slaves. Everything was done at the discretion of the master. Gwen, along with many others, including family members, took the long walk up to the big white house.

When everyone, except the maimed, feeble and youngest children, had been gathered in front of the big house the master, taking his time, and sat in a chair, asked for a letter to be brought to him. One of his supervisors went inside to retrieve the said item and eventually returned holding a rolled up piece of paper. After receiving the letter, the master stood up, steadied himself and before doing anything else looked out at the gathered throng of slaves. In the past, at similar gatherings, he would have shown a sense of satisfaction across his reddened face. However, on this occasion, he seemed sad.

Gwen and the others knew that it was bad news for the master, and although jubilant inside, she was not showing her delight for others to see. After all, she thought, with a wry little smile on her face, she wanted to see the man squirm. At that point, Gwen noticed that his eyes fell upon the vast plantation and slowly surveyed the cane fields, the boiling houses and the small shacks that doubled as sleeping quarters and place of abode for five hundred 'workers'. Once, Gwen was told, the master would continually remind friends and visitors that his slaves "knew their place".

At one time, remembered Gwen, when the plantation was at its most productive, more than one thousand slaves worked the land. That was until the new draconian apprenticeship rules came into force. The master had seen those rules as the beginning of the end for his family's lust for fortune and fame. Gwen was only too aware that the British Empire had profited handsomely off the backs millions of decent people who had lived through the indignity of "slavery". She felt the pain and hatred welled up inside her.

Eventually, the master, with that saddened look upon his face, addressed the crowd of economically and politically destitute, and sometimes broken, people that had gathered to hear the news. He held up the document and told everyone that the apprenticeship system had come to an end and that they were free and could go wherever they wanted to go. This was a big surprise to some people, and they looked on aghast and at each other. That was then immediately followed by a crescendo of raised voices as each individual tried to make sense of what they had heard. Some people who had not fully heard what was said asked for clarification from their neighbours. Others were glad and openly celebrated their new-found freedom from enslavement. To them, it had been a long time coming. Many were crying and some even rolled around on the ground as if possessed by some evil spirit. A few were already running to their abodes to retrieve their meagre belongings before immediately leaving the plantation. In their minds, thought Gwen, they had no intention of staying any longer since they were now declared free and they wanted the place to become a distance memory.

In some parts of the crowd there seemed to have been mayhem taking place as some people pleaded on bended knees to be kept on to work the plantation. Still, others were furious with the antics of people who were now free and, Gwen recognised, that they should carry that badge with pride. Gwen chuckled a little and thought how funny it was that a few words could cause so many different emotions to come to the fore. In Gwen's mind, it could also be seen that people who were once in the same situation and experienced the same indignities and cruelty, still all acted so differently on hearing the news.

The master looked even more solemn that before and asked for silence from those who remained while watching a small procession of what were effectively ex-apprentices about to walk off the property. Some stood still, and others returned to hear what was to be said. There was an eerie silence in the expectant air that drifted across the plantation, and it must have seemed to some people that the earth had stood still. Gwen realised that many people had once more become silent and were wondering what else could the master had to say that granted such solemnity. He continued by telling all that had ears to listen, and that the plantation would be closing down and that he and his wife and children were returning back to England within the week. He promptly repeated the self-same message for everyone to hear.

Gwen noticed that that had come as a huge shock to some people. Many of those people had already concluded that they had nothing to do and nowhere to go if the plantation closed its doors. More weeping and wailing was heard from a small number of people. At that point many people stood paralysed to the spot and some were numbed with fear. Others looked at the place they had called home since birth, and where their ancestors had worked and had been buried. Many people had never even ventured outside the gates of the plantation and were visibly shaken by the news. After a short while, some made it clear that they were staying and even sat down immovable on the ground, and others lay prostrate. They contested that the plantation was the only home that they had ever known. Disbelief had them by the throats and was refusing to let go its vice-like grip.

Gwen watched it all unfold. She had known that the day would come when the plantation would finally close its doors to everything and everyone. As she watched each person's reaction, she was sad for those individuals who had nowhere to go and those who had never been outside the boundaries of the plantation. Up until the announcement the plantation had been their medicine, family, shelter, clothing and food. Luckily, some people had gained trades over the years, including those who looked after horses, made barrels, sewed shoes, made clothes, and so on. There were even freed slaves who had been plying their trades on the plantation who would need to go elsewhere for work.

The master had left the yard and re-entered the big house. Many of the house slaves followed as there time at the plantation would end when they would leave the following week. The turmoil outside would continue for a while longer until the reality of the situation would dawn on them and they drifted back to homes that were soon to be empty shells, gathered their belongings, continued to cry, slept for a time and eventually moved out.

Gwen considered her own future and was joined by others who had sought her out for guidance. Over time she had gained some vital skills that she had kept secret from those people who would have been detrimental to herself and her family. Only a few people had been told or benefited from the exceptional skills that she had gained. She then made it known to others that she had been a liaison between trusted slaves still on the plantation and the Maroons who had established thriving and new communities up in the hills. Gwen, who was both wise and shrewd in her choice of acquaintances, told them how they could join the people known as the Maroons. Gwen then took from beneath her bed a small pouch which contained a letter. She read the contents to the dismay of some of the onlookers who did not know that she could read. There were no surprises on the faces of the trusted few that she had brought into her circle of influence. From that day Gwen became their teacher and passage to an even greater freedom for themselves and their descendants.

Gwen was that woman who had been taught to read and write and sold by the master to another plantation.

Childhood and Innocence

River Come Down

Granny could "smell" rain before it had a chance to fall in the district. It was something I tried but could never do. Maybe you had to have a particular kind of nose to smell rain. Or you had learned from somebody how to do it. Mr Jones from up the hill was on the road and called out to Granny. He wanted to know when it would rain.

"It soon come", Granny would reply.

I still don't understand what that meant. Uncle Bertie had left the house two days before, and told somebody that he "soon come"; and he don't return since then. My bigger brother, we call him Plenty, always telling me that he going up the road some mornings and "soon come" but he never reach home until night almost catch him out the road. I don't know what he always doing up the road. But I hear that a young woman catch his eye in the neighbouring district. Sometimes Granny would be more specific and tell people the rain just over the hill. Then in a few hours, it appeared.

The funny thing about it was that nobody started to make haste, walk faster or run until the rain start fall. Years later many people would let me know that it was a Caribbean thing. I concluded long ago that it was much more than that and put it all down to the hot climate and the need to conserve energy. That's a puzzling thing with our people. I wondered whether every district was the same and found out they were.

Dreams of Freedom

I stayed in a place call Golden Pass with Uncle Freddie last month and before rainfall everybody just going about their business as usual. I heard people telling others that "rain soon come", and the other would just reply with a "yeah, soh mi hear to", and they would continue doing whatever they were doing. On some occasions, you would see somebody running, just before the rain came down, or during the first drops, to take their clothes off the washing line.

One thing was for sure, it seemed as if everybody wanted to be in their own house when rain was falling. That is something else I could never understand when I was growing up. While playing out with my friends, and in their homes, Granny would call, send a message or came to take me home. It was like other people's homes were not good enough. She would also tell my friends to go home because "rain soon come". Granny never went anywhere when she knows that rain was about to fall. She would always hurry back long before the rain could even be seen in the distance. This was never the case for some people since there were always a few "brave" souls that preferred to spend their time, rain or shine, propping up the local rum bar when the rain came. Their gamble was probably deliberate given their "liquid pastime" because some firmly believed that maybe a foreigner, visiting for the first time, may get caught in the rain and run for shelter in the rum bar. It would be a good time to get a drink or two.

It was the storm season, and care had to be taken by everybody in the district. Each person would be out in their yards and maybe packing up their belongings and making sure that what could not be brought indoors was well secured outdoors. Also, there were some poorer people in the district whose makeshift kitchens were out in the open air and they had to bring into the house all their plates, pots, pans and other belongings. This was especially the case when heavy rain or the stormy weather was on its way.

Mr Elijah donkey looked at him as if to say "why you don't just let me come in the house and done'. Mr Elijah was a wise man and knew the value of a donkey in the district. The donkey represented ownership of an important means of transport. It meant not carrying the little you can on your head, but carrying most of what you could on the donkey. Too many trips made a man weary. The donkey was a constant companion and whether you complained or talked the hind leg off the donkey it always listened and never answered back. I saw it with my own eyes. So Mr Elijah used to complain until even the devil stop listen as he went about his own business each day. The donkey also represented money. Mr Elijah would plant yam, dasheen, cocoa, bananas and anything else he thought could sell. His trusty donkey was always loaded and walking by his side wherever he went.

Mr Elijah would say that "Di donkey better than goat. Yu seh, goat never carry anything and always a eat."

On one occasion Mr Elijah took the goats into the bush where his hard work had been done. When he was tired from his labour he would just sit back down and rest, and sometimes fall asleep. But many times goats just knew how to make a man go crazy. They would wander off into the bush for hours and no matter how a man call they don't seem to answer. It could take hours to find them and by that time a man could become angrier, hungry and too tired to look for them.

The bus was late, and Miss Etty didn't know why. So she asked her neighbour Miss Violet why the bus late, but she didn't know either.

So Miss Violet asked the same question of her neighbour Miss Nessie. Soon the whole district asking the same question and nobody could give an answer. However, sometimes when the bus is really late coming from town some people claim to know why even though it was pure speculation. These people existed to get other people upset. One person would tell the other person across the road or the neighbouring house that they think the bus breakdown, just like it did a few times before. Another would call out that it was just the driver late as usual. Yet another may consider that fight break out, or somebody didn't want to pay, and police had to come and draw their guns to stop any arguing and fighting. That was all and good until one brave, or mainly stupid, person would open their mouth and mention the unthinkable.

"Suppose the bus turnover like it did three years ago. You know how much people get kill?" asked Joseph, without expecting an answer.

Then there would be amongst everybody for a little while before Short Foot Sandra would want to know why Joseph had to mention that old time story. She would start to argue with Joseph and get ready to fight the man. However, others would start to go back in their memories and talk about the incident that killed a whole lot people and injured so many. Martha always cried at the mere mention of the accident that left her husband dead.

"The bus too full", said yet another person.

Another would dispute that statement and reply that the driver not looking where he was going because of the rain. At that point, everyone, except Joseph who started the argument and had gone into his house, just looked up to the sky.

"Rain soon come," was on everyone's mind.

The bus came. I heard the horn, as the huge vehicle hurtled up the hill. It was still a clear distance down the narrow and winding road that led into the small community. Drivers blew their horns for any reason at all. Sometimes they just warning oncoming traffic that they were coming; and other times horns get blown to attract people attention – especially when friends meandering up and down the roads. Leroy, a driver from the district, would always blow his horn to let the family know he was passing by. And he had a lot of family along the route. However, most times the drivers just let people who travelling that day know the bus was coming, and it was time to leave the house or else they get left behind. On many occasions, such as any oncoming storm, drivers would let people know that the vehicle was both safe and at the same time the driver was racing against time to be home before its swirling cloak covered them and everything else.

There would be sighs of relief, but words continued their exchange between neighbours about Joseph's earlier behaviour. Then the community would drift back into its daily activities once more. However, I was never certain about why people found it so easy to become aggressive with their neighbours over something as simple as the arrival, or non-arrival of a bus. Interestingly, Joseph would remain unrepentant and wait for the next time. I believe that he was a lonely old man and need something to break up his day. Maybe he had troubles of his own and enjoyed stirring up trouble just to listen to other people's woes rather than think about his own.

The rain hides behind blankets of menacing clouds in the sky. If you could look across the valley to the mountains, you could also see the rain as it stretched its menacing fingers in the direction of the district. Everyone could see the gradual darkening of the sky as it went from the blue and fluffy clouds a few hours before to the grey and misty appearance that would be expressed as happiness or sadness on people's faces. On one hand, nature taught everyone to depend on rain for life to continue. This made people happy. But, on the other hand, the rain put a stop to some people. And that made some quite sad and angry too. The trusty sun, much like a bad boy in school, had been sent away by the coming storm to some mysterious place not known to man.

As a child, I was always fascinated by the coming and going of the moon and sun each day; but before hurricanes and storms, everything seemed much more serious. The marching rain soldiers were on their way as darkness take hold and little else could be seen in the distance. Some people, such as Granny, could smell the rain a long time before it appeared and so were forewarned of the coming deluge. Also, Granny just took it all in her stride. She would tell you that rain and storm just another blessing from God. Earlier, over the horizon, some of the bigger people who already been through bad storm and hurricanes before noticed the dark clouds and commented on times gone by and the aftermath of those events. As the invasion got closer and closer, appearing below the clouds was what resembled silvery sheets falling from the sky. On some occasions, the rain came with a couple of friends – lightning and thunder.

I could see animals and people scurrying for shelter. The rain, much like an orchestra, would begin slowly. At first, there would be a mysterious silence before a kind of lazy breeze that blew from over the hills. The light breeze came like a friend, but clearly brought with it a few guests. If it were a storm, you would see the lightning and hear thunder in the distance. This eventually became more audible as if a message was being sent to say that it was calling by for awhile, and it may be staying for dinner. To me, at the time, it felt like a veiled threat that simply became reality too quickly. During the waiting time, most people in the district, after making final preparations, sat around as if awaiting an attack from an enemy force. Then the rain came.

The first time storm comes, it sounds like the pitter-patter of tiny feet running over trees until it became a crescendo of sound. As it came down, individual raindrops began shaking hands with the leaves of trees, and as they bowed they begin calling their friends to the meeting that in turn would become turn a small flood. As individual raindrops became partnerships, they ran from dancing leaves and down to the thirsty ground where ground harmonies join the rising crescendo. Dried leaves and parched earth all allowed their own joyfulness to join become part of the growing orchestra compelled to create and confined by nothing.

This time, it was a storm, and each raindrop happily joined together with others to produce, at first, small veins of oxygen-enriched nectar for the previously dry and unyielding soil. Soon, they all became streams of gushing water tumbling down from the hills above and lashing the patiently waiting valley below. On either side of my Granny's small house run trenches to divert the oncoming torrent along channels and away from the house. Granny's house stood on stilts – large wooden posts – that held the small building above ground so as to allow water to run beneath. The zinc-top roof became part of the orchestra that came to both entertain and threaten. Gutters captured rainwater and directed them to an empty barrel behind the house. The old and rickety construction of everything, wholly inadequate if a strong storm or hurricane hit the area, had to be questioned. Small streams that formed had become tiny rivulets, and very soon even rivers were overflowing and threatening the livelihood, and lives, of residents in the valleys below.

As a child, I remembered the rainfall so vividly, as it fell upon the zinc-top roof of Granny's house. I loved the rain and always looked forward to its coming with a significant amount of delight and expectation. My grandmother's house had the grand total of one bedroom! Inside there was a bed, a table and one wooden chair that had been made by my uncle. I was never sure why there was a chair in the bedroom. I was told that it was for guests, but the veranda was so small that people sat on the steps or stood, and nobody ever went inside the house except my grandmother and me. When it rained, it was like music to my ears. In fact, rainfall was the sweetest thing in my childhood. When the rain came, I would curl up in the bed (or sometimes underneath), with a spoonful of wet sugar (kept in a jar or tin on the table), listen intently to the lovely and soothing rhythm played on the zinc roof, and eventually falling asleep.

Whenever there was a storm falling asleep was not so easy to do because of the loudness of the thunder, the lightning and howling winds. In that case, I would usually curl up under Granny's bed and remained as still and for as long as possible - listening with fear and trepidation to the wind and thunder outside. It always felt as if someone was dismantling the world, including Granny's house, as it shook, creaked and suffered heavy blows throughout the storm. With Granny, I always felt safe since she was on the bed above me and sometimes called to find out whether I was asleep as yet. It was never easy, but sometimes I did eventually fall asleep. Granny never slept during storms or hurricanes.

In many places, after the storm had passed, the ground became very slippery and sometimes extremely dangerous to walk upon because some areas became quite muddy. Kitchens were not usually joined to the houses and were more likely to suffer damage and needed immediate attention. After storms, many homes and other buildings were blown down, crops were ruined, roadways washed away, and many people needed help to rebuild their lives. Granny's house was secure and had seen many storms. Some people came to shelter in her home until they could be rebuilt. It sometimes became quite crowded in the little house. Granny's house, but for a few minor repairs and a lifting roof, was still relatively intact. The yard was sheltered by big sturdy coconut and breadfruit trees. Even though this was a good thing, there was always the chance that the trees could have fallen on the house. Granny never let that worry her as she was usually heard to say that everything was in God's hands. The kitchen was not so lucky. It had to be re-built.

Unfortunately, several people lost their lives in the district during that storm. It was a sombre affair in all cases as nine-nights (visiting with the victims' families until the funeral) were kept and funerals held. Auntie Blanche died when her house collapsed during the storm, and she was not found until the following day. Part of Joseph's house fell on his leg, but he survived and limped around for awhile, and could be found drinking rum at every funeral and arguing with whoever he could find.

As a child, playing in the rain was heavenly. However, storms and hurricanes were different according to my Granny. And she was right. Instead, after the worst of the storm had died down I would race out of the house, across the yard and to where water continued to rush down from the hills passing through Granny's property and into the river about a mile below. This was the greatest fun for children growing up in the countryside. As I mentioned before, children were not yet accustomed to noticing the downside of such events. That was for adults to worry about. Children enjoyed the difference that such calamities caused, the new river banks and waters were always something that brought out their positivity and creativity.

Other young children and I would play for hours in the mud and water. Sometimes we would see who could jump the furthest across swollen gullies. Many times we would fall in, but nobody cared too much about that. Other times we would gather sticks, identified our personal 'stick', each threw them into the rushing waters at the same time and followed them down the fast flowing streams to see which stick had travelled the furthest. The winner was always jubilant. We never stopped until everyone was tired, dirty and hungry. Or at least until Granny called me.

Kingston Life

When I was young Kingston was a fabulously vibrant and busy place that filled my senses with excitement and awe. I was always drawn to the vehicles and particularly what was called at the time the 'fish-tail cars', which were American cars that looked so big, flashy and elegant. There began my fascination with cars. I was also bombarded with music from everywhere. Each shop would have their own music playing as you passed by and in those times, before Reggae, Ska and Rock Steady were in vogue. I loved the place. I was seven years old and had the protection of my mother and other relatives living and working in Kingston.

Before visiting my mother in Kingston, I used to live with my grandmother in the country where I went to school, had my friends and generally ran around my father's property. He had left for a foreign land to work to support the family back in Jamaica. When I was, according to my mother, "too much for you granny to manage", she would send for me to join her in Kingston. Very early in the morning my grandmother would put me on the bus to Kingston and cried as she did it. I was always sad to leave my friends, especially my best friend Roy, and sometimes I cried too. But my tears would soon be dried as I enjoyed watching all the trees, houses and bright colours go by. I wanted to see my mother, but the ride was much too long for an energetic child, and I definitely did not enjoy that experience.

On arriving in Kingston, my mother would meet me at the bus terminus with a big smile, and I was happy to see her too. However, as the days went by, she was always too busy to be with me, so I made up my own games, threw stones at people and hid, teased other children and caused a nuisance in everything I did. I was a child and wanted a challenge. Today, having children myself, I realise that they need direction and support from adults since they are always ready and willing to explore and question the strange new world around them.

Even back then Kingston could be a very dangerous place for a child like me, filled with inquisitiveness, bravado and imagination. On one occasion I stayed upstairs and spat at a passing soldier. My aim must have been good because he looked up and hastily ran to complain to my mother's employer. He was none too pleased but managed to calm down the soldier who then left the premises. My mother's employer was not happy with her. I was punished and was not allowed near the window anymore, and that was not good for a child like me. It felt like I was destined to be sent back to my grandmother in the country.

Children mostly see the fun side in what happens when they are young. This was especially the case when it rained. Me and Alice, another seven years old, would take off all our clothes and dance around, on the roof - in the pouring rain. We felt free and splashed around until adults got in the way. This was never behaviour that my mother enjoyed since Alice was her employer's daughter. She feared to lose her job as a domestic within the household, and she was determined to keep me on a tight leash. However, this was not always possible, and my inquisitive mind and high energy would often get me into even more trouble. For instance, my mother's employer had a shop downstairs and sold many different products, including buttons, cloth, sewing materials and peanuts by the bag.

As you probably gathered, Alice was always my accomplice in mischief making. Behind the shop was a poverty-stricken area known as 'back-a-wall'. Here, desperately poor people lived and eked out a meagre living for themselves. Most people dwelling there seemed as if they were verging on daily starvation. We, as children, wanted to help and therefore became charity workers for a little while by handing out peanuts to the occupants of the area. This was done through a hole in the wall close by where the peanuts were kept. This went on every day for around a week, and by then several bags of peanuts had been shared out. Eventually, Alice's father found out, and he was more than furious. We were both banned from entering the shop. So, I was prohibited from going to the upstairs window, the roof and now the shop. However, this did not dampen our enthusiasm as we found other interesting, and apparently mischievous, things to do before I was quickly sent back to my grandmother in the country.

When I was in Kingston, much of my time was spent with my blind cousin who lived in Jones Town. When things had gotten too much for my mother, she would put me on the number seventeen bus that was passing from Parade which took me to Jones Town. We had already visited my cousin together, and I had already spent time walking around the tenement yard and playing with the other children. On one occasion we all decided to leave the yard so as to go out on the road. Before we could do that, I heard a voice from inside.

"You children must stay inside the yard. Nothing no out a street for you. Come back inside". It was my cousin Andrew.

I did not think much of the incident at the time until I went to stay with him. The first time I visited my cousin alone my mother put me on the bus and told the driver where to put me off. My mother mentioned Andrew by name and then told the driver that the man was blind. The bus driver smiled and said that he knew him well. I was all alone on the bus for a little while watching the houses, the many shops, the people, the cars and all the bright lights as they went by. The bus driver put me off where Andrew lived and pointed to the yard. I made my way to the tenement yard.

Cousin Andrew was waiting for me. I never noticed his blindness unless he asked me to find something he had mislaid. However, that was rare since he knew where he had put everything in the house. He also cooked, and that was always nice. My best memory of this loving blind man was when we visited the town centre, and he would lead me by the hand along the crowded streets. Cousin Andrew always warned me to mind my step and the kerbs as we stepped up and down. Crossing the roads with Cousin Andrew was fun since he seemed to know when the vehicles were coming, where from, what kind of vehicle and he even described them to me. He would say to me "keep quiet bwoy make me hear what a gwaan." And I would watch him as he listened intently. Then after a little while, he would speak.

"Come, cross now. And hurry up, the number seventeen bus a come." How did he know that? I was fascinated with my cousin, and although he was blind and living in a busy city, I was never afraid. Today, when I think about our trips, it felt so amazing. And I always felt safe with Cousin Andrew.

On many occasions when my mother wanted a little peace and quiet to get on with her work, she would leave me with Cousin Egbert, who worked by the train line. It was not far from where my mother worked, and we usually got up early in the morning and walked to where he would be waiting for us. He would greet us with a big toothy grin, and he had a husky but quiet voice. He didn't work in a building, but he had a street cart which he steered using what looked like a vehicle's steering wheel as he pushed it up and down the roads around the train line. He sold cane juice to passersby. Cousin Egbert's cane juice was delicious. After making the juice, with lemons added for tanginess, he would make sure that he packed it with ice which was deep within the street cart. This was a great business since people were always hot and thirsty as the sun would beat down each day upon the bustling city. However, as a child, it was just so good to be out in the open all day. Sometimes I played with other children in the area, but Cousin Egbert would also spend time telling me stories, and when I was tired I fell asleep and lay down in the shade near the cart.

Staying with my mother at her place of work had become less exciting for me as time went by since she was always working and I wasn't allowed to play with Alice or any of the other children. However, when she had a day off work, we would go shopping and walking in King Street, Duke Street, Coronation market, Parade and many places. However, at night we also had time to talk, and she would let me know about Kingston and the people that she met every day. Across the road, every Friday and Saturday night, there was always a dance and music would be played loudly. My mother and I shared a room, and we could see and hear all the people going and coming from the dance and the latest Ska and Rock Steady tunes would play on into the night. One song that would become a favourite during that time, and ever since was "Simmer Down" by The Wailers.

One thing about being a small child is that you had a chance to taste all kinds of food and drink. I always had a sweet tooth and enjoyed eating bulla cakes and sucking on paradise plum. Next door to where my mother worked there was a shop that sold Toto (a kind of small bun), Pepsi and Canada Dry. Since I had no money and my mother could not afford to give me money every day, the other older children, including the employer's children, would buy for me. And when I finished one drink I would check the inside of the bottle top to find out whether it was green or red. If it were green, I would return them to the shop, with the bottle, and I got a free drink! Every day people would be queuing outside the store to buy Canada Dry. I had no money most of the time, so I just watched everyone else's disappointment or excitement.

Kingston was never the same place to me when I returned as an adult many years later. The place I had grown to love as a child became a disappointment to me as a man. Returning there today, as an adult fills me with a deep, lingering and painful fear. To me, it seems like the friendliness and honesty that once existed had all but disappeared. On my most recent visit, I was even more shocked to find so many people sleeping on the streets. Kingston had also been left to the elements, and it looks as if people have given up and just decide to survive, and they had lost their pride in Jamaica.

In fact, I want my happy childhood memories of Kingston to remain with me forever. Every time I think about that town in the early nineteen sixties, it fills me with the sounds, sights, tastes, smells and even the touch of the place. Sometimes adults choose to live in the present and the harsh realities of life. However, I prefer to drift away to a time and place that continues to be one of peace, laughter and smiles in times of troubles.

I remembered that when it was time to go back to the country I was usually in floods of tears. And yet deep down I knew how much

Dreams of Freedom

I had missed Roy, my school friend; my grandmother and her shouting at me; running through the bushes and climbing trees, and visiting my other grandmother and grandfather up in the hills. Those thoughts always made me happy once more. However, leaving Kingston always left a bitter-sweet taste in my mouth.

Dreams, Struggles and Love

The Gathering

The time had gone so quickly, and the yard had not yet been swept to Aunt Rose's satisfaction. Nobody had thought to do it, and the guests were on their way to the house. The twins had already swept it earlier in the day, but it needed sweeping again. Aunt Rose suddenly appeared from the house wearing her best frock and a pearl necklace and called out for the twins to do the job. This was not a time to dawdle, thought, Aunt Rose. However, when the twins could not be found she angrily took the broom and swept the yard herself. She was sweeping up in her best frock and looking like Cinderella about to go to the ball. Aunt Rose was not a happy woman as she got down to the task of making the yard spotless for the soon to arrive guests.

Old Man Taylor just stood and watched as Aunt Rose was frantically sweeping everywhere that she could find a little trash or twigs from the low-hanging trees that were dotted around the yard. He was in the way, and Aunt Rose gently nudged him aside before standing back satisfied that the yard was as spotless as she wanted it to be. At that point, the twins returned to ask her what she had wanted. She set her hand to box them both but thought better of it as the guests were close to arriving and the food was almost ready.

Not too long afterwards people began arriving and Aunt Rose, with her customary enormous smile on her face, set about meeting and greeting each one. It was the dry season, the sun was really hot. People, as they arrived, sat on chairs and other makeshift benches out in the yard underneath trees. Miss Jenny kept on looking up into the trees since she had a dislike of lizards. A few people, the early ones, sat on the veranda to rest their weary legs. Many had travelled from quite a distance such as Miss Bertha and her husband, Tom. They had been walking for almost one hour in the hot sun, and the way that they were both dressed anyone would have thought that they were going to Sunday morning service. Tom had donned his hat to keep off the sun, and Bertha had brought her umbrella. Along the way, they rested beneath the cool shades of several big trees. Miss Bertha was about seventy years of age, although she never shared her real age with anyone.

Uncle Benjie, Aunt Rose's cousin-in-law and potential suitor, brought a fruit cake which he said had been made by his sister Beryl who was not able to attend on account of her bad foot. The suitor thing did not work for Aunt Rose after she had noticed how many 'girls' he had proposed to over the past few years. She considered him too common for her sophisticated taste. Aunt Rose thanked him and took the cake, putting it to one side for the guests to have after dinner.

Eventually, the other guests arrived, including "Miss Lateness" herself Wilhelmina Duncan-Blessed. So Aunt Rose and her daughter Vashti served dinner for everyone. It was curry goat and rice, done the Aunt Rose way. She had bought a goat especially for the occasion from Old Man Taylor, who she considered to be the meanest man in the district. However, she was always impressed by his money handling skills. He was never a man to waste it and he was honest to a fault. She had already decided not to pay him until the gathering had finished. He had protested about her decision, but Aunt Rose would have none of it. Although totally against his principles, Old Man Taylor agreed. He had a soft spot for Aunt Rose.

After dinner and when everyone had eaten their fill, had cake and drank heartily, Aunt Rose thanked them all for attending her very special occasion. She reminded them that life had been hard for some years and that she had tried to make the most of what she had. She mentioned her beloved husband who had died several years before and then went on to state the purpose of the gathering. Her son, James, the one who loved the young ladies, was leaving for England in a few days time. He had announced it to her only a week ago, and it was all a mother could do for her one son. Even though she tried to hide it, everyone could see both pride and sadness written upon her face. There were no tears. Aunt Rose never showed her emotions when in company and she was certainly not going to do it then.

People in the district were usually afraid of her because she was a woman who told you exactly what she wanted you to hear. Aunt Rose never ever minced her words. To this woman, born into hardship and poverty, a spade was a spade. Some people called her callous because she was always happy to speak her mind. However, she never cared about what people thought about her. This was sometimes her downfall and especially living in a small community where everyone knew everybody else's business. If you wanted to hear the truth you would go to Aunt Rose and she would just tell you the truth - as she saw it! If uncertain about something, she would not say a word. She had to have the facts before anything came out of her mouth. In fact, many people called her inquisitive when she probed them for facts to support her believe. It was never an easy life for Aunt Rose in the district - but she loved every minute of it.

As she spoke about her son and the things she had gone through to get him to where he was, she looked in the direction of Old Man

Taylor for support but turned away when he failed to notice the hint. Old Man Taylor was an unusual man in that he hardly ever spoke. When he did speak it would be to ask for something. Aunt Rose liked that part of his personality since she never enjoyed being defied by any man. This was a man that she could twist around her little finger, and he would not say a word except to ask for his money! If only, she wondered, he would notice her.

Old Man Taylor, not really so old, got his name from the way he walked like an old man. He has walked that way ever since he was a young boy and the name stuck. After Maas Jerry, Aunt Rose's husband died, Old Man Taylor had always helped out where he could in the yard. Even the children and grandchildren saw him as father and grandfather. Aunt Rose never saw it that way. "Old Man Taylor just want somewhere to hang his hat, lay his head and get a little warmth", Aunt Rose would be heard to say on many occasions. She has shown little interest in another man since the death of her husband. She always joked that she would die an old maid before any other man touched her. And so, all the other eligible men in the district stayed away from her. Some because of what she had said, but mostly because they just could not manage her. In fact, only Old Man Taylor realised that she was mostly bark and little bite where he was concerned. And at his time of life, he was quite happy to bear the bite!

Aunt Rose wished her son all the best for his journey to "foreign" as he sat watching all the guests that surrounded him. Aunt Rose and others then tried to encourage him to give a short speech. Although a shy man before a crowd, James obediently stood up, surveyed with some nervousness the faces of those people watching and waiting to hear him speak, thanked everyone for coming before promptly sitting back down. That was indeed a short speech thought Aunt Rose. She continued on his behalf, but before anyone else could notice James quickly slinked away into the undergrowth that surrounded the yard. He just simply melted into the many trees that stood like guards around the yard. Aunt Rose was disgusted with him and showed it on her face until she sat down again.

Not much longer after James had left several women from the district turned up at the yard. They were looking for James. They told Aunt Rose that they had heard that he was going away to "foreign" and had come to bid him farewell. Immediately Aunt Rose asked one girl to leave her yard. The girl kissed her teeth and did as she was told. She turned and walked away. The other two girls seemed nervous around Aunt Rose. She did not even look at one of the girls and ignored her as she beckoned the other to be seated near the veranda. Obviously, James was nowhere to be seen and the young woman sat a little shyly amongst the other guests. She was offered dinner but refused and instead had some cake and a drink.

James, coyly looking around as he walked, conveniently returned after the girls had left and as the other guests were leaving too. Most people had already gone, and the yard was looking a little bare after the gathering. It seemed that James was hiding from several of the girls who had visited. Aunt Rose knew the reason but said nothing. She had already had her say a few weeks earlier when she compared him to his father. Maas Jerry, she had told him, loved the girls, and it became his downfall she told James. She had made it clear to him that there was no point in hiding from some of those women, as the deed had already been done. Aunt Rose knew about the children that had been fathered by her son. However, James was intelligent and decided that leaving for foreign was his escape from the many women that had collared him to support them and the children. At that point, the mother of the twins came looking for James. He quickly dashed into the undergrowth once more before she could have a chance to speak with him. Aunt Rose knew that those two never talked but instead shouted and argued. Nobody listened to anybody, and such relationships were doomed to failure. She only put up with the woman because she had manners to her and she was the mother of the adorable twins - her grandchildren. The twin's mother greeted her but soon turned away since James had disappeared once more.

Aunt Rose was not happy with the antics of her son but realised that James was now a big man. As she considered the enormity of the situation - that her little boy was leaving Jamaica for a foreign land - tears welled up in her eyes. She hid this from everyone for awhile but soon it could not be hidden anymore, and she started to bawl. The remaining guests looked around and towards Aunt Rose as she cried and wheeled around and wailed. Few people could believe that this was the woman who hardly ever showed weakness before others. And yet it was true. She was inconsolable for a time as several ladies, although tentative at first, made their way to comfort her. However, on each occasion, she told them to go away. Each woman, not knowing what to do, returned, unsuccessful in their attempts, to their respective places. This woman with the tough exterior was crying like a baby and letting everyone know that her little boy was leaving her.

Eventually, after what seemed like such a long time and so many tears, she was comforted by, of all people, Old Man Taylor. This was a huge surprise to everyone as she buried her head in the man's chest and hugs him too. The man had no choice but to hug her back. His surprise quickly turned into a huge smile as he looked around rather more confidently at the onlookers. In his mind, it seemed that at last, he had found a place to hang his hat and lay his head. Aunt Rose looked at him with tears in her eyes and smiled.

Nana

My name is Richie, and I am on holiday in my dad's place of birth. A place in the Caribbean called Jamaica. It's a small island in the sun where he left to look for his treasures far across the sea. I am almost twenty years old, and my father thought that I needed to spend my birthday with my grandmother. However, he said nothing about the countryside! The place is way up in the hills, very bushy and there was no television. This was a million miles from the urban sprawl into which I was born - a big place called London. It was so quiet here – and hot! Where I am from it could get really cold for most of the year. This place seemed so much like a wild and unforgiving place. The people are nice and friendly, but they are also quite strange. They look at me as if they want to eat me - and those are the guys! The girls seem quite nice too - until they speak; I have no idea what they are saying. They smile a lot, and when you talk to them, some can be silent. Maybe they don't understand me – I certainly don't get them.

Papa said that many people living in the district are my family and that they would all be so glad to see me. However, I don't know them, so how will they know me? The guys out here wear some really funny clothes. There must be some designer outlets in the towns where they can buy better clothes. Where I'm from, you have to look your best – dress to impress. Here they walk around in ripped and tatty clothes most of the day. However, in the evening when going out to party, they do dress well. I saw a few of them passing the gate and going to some dance further up the road. They asked me to go with them, and I said no. I have only been here two days so there is time yet to get to know what people do for fun.

It's been a sweltering day, and so I am sitting at the back of the house where it was cooler. Papa said that there are about two acres of land around the house. It seems like a forest of trees and bushes to me. Right now, I'm looking out for wild animals crashing through the undergrowth and eating me alive. So I am just watching and listening with great attention. Papa and Jake, my brother, went into the town, and I decided to stay with Nana.

"Come tek up deh clothes dem fah mi" hollered Nana from the veranda.

I heard her shrill small voice and came running from the back of the house as quickly as I could. She was tottering down the steps that led into the yard where the clothes were hanging.

"Noh mek dem get wet, it out fi rain", she uttered as she picked her way gingerly down the last of the steps.

She pointed to the clothes on the washing line and then to the basket lying on the ground next to the steps leading up to the house. The clothes had been painstakingly washed by hand and were put out to dry just forty-five minutes earlier. They were almost dry.

I would have left them there, but it seemed like to Nana that would have been sacrilege. As I was coming around into the yard, I could see that the sunlight had left the sky. My father had told me once that Nana could smell rain in the air - long before the rain even touched down. I know from my studies that the atmosphere was always sending messages to our senses, but few ever heeded its warning. I tried to smell the air, but to no avail. She probably had a different kind of nose to me. I preferred the smell of delicious chicken and rice that Mama cooked on Sundays. However, I could see that there were dark clouds in the distance.

I had already unpegged most of the clothes when Nana had come down the steps and into the yard.

She then reached for the last piece of clothes saying, "mek mi tek it down mi'self for unno yung people too slow".

I understood some of what she was saying, but the rest sounded Greek to me. Mama and Papa sometimes spoke that way at home – especially when they were quarrelling. I looked at Nana and shook my head, and then a smile would burst out on my face. Nana noticed this.

"A wey yu a luk soh glad fah? Yu tink de ole lady funny?" she enquired.

"I think you are great, Nana", I said as I turned to take the basket of clothes into the house.

She just kissed her teeth and said "G'wey fram mi, yu too bad!"

I could almost detect affection in her voice. I wanted to help her, but she would have none of it.
She said, "wen yu all gaan I afi to do it m'self".

As I walked up the steps and looked out beyond the road, I could see that the sky was still getting darker. The sun was taking a break, and the clouds were left to play. Nana took her time going up the steps so I asked: "do you want help?" She looked my way and said nothing but continued her journey up the steps. She was so frail and so stubborn that it was difficult not to go out to help her inside. I did it anyway and held her hand as she mounted the last step. She looked at me without saying a word. Since arriving here, I have noticed that she does not normally ask for help to get around. I guess that she had been doing everything herself for her whole life, and now that she was alone she found it difficult to ask for help.

My father said that her life had been a hard one. In fact, she raised all her children by herself after Grandpa passed away prematurely. She was now in her late seventies (few people knew her real age, but some thought that she was over eighty years old) and determined to live independently. That is what she had been used to. I thought that the rain would reach her before she got up the stairs. She eventually entered the veranda and fumbled with the lock on the grill as she tried to close it. Again I went to her rescue. She looked at me and said "yu tink sey becas mi ole mi kyan duh nuttin?"

I didn't fully understand what she meant, but when she saw that I hadn't moved away, she gave up and started toward the house.

Before she went in she turned and said, "yu know 'ow long mi deh pon dis eart'?"

She continued, "yu tink yu cudda run and jump roun' like mi wen mi young?".

She then entered the house – not expecting an answer from me. I said nothing for awhile, even though I wanted to find out more about her life. I had never truly thought about what Papa went through when he was young. It must have been very difficult growing up in poverty. Papa sometimes cried when he talked about his past. Then after listening, Mama would say something funny that made him laugh. It was then that heard Nana from inside the house saying something like the clothes had not dried properly. Nana was so funny. I decided to go inside the house and between us, we hung the clothes out on the veranda. Nana smiled at me and held my hand before letting go and returning to her room.

As Nana had said, you could smell the rain as it arrived. I am sure that I did before the first drop could be seen. Nana told me what to do before the rain came and we worked well as a team to get it all done. Everything had been readied – the chickens were roosting, the drums for catching rainwater were uncovered, and Nana was inside the house. Then the rain started its eerie magic and began slowly with small drops on the leaves of the nearby trees and bushes. As each drop kissed a leaf, it would in turn dance around with joy. At first, there was no sound. It began by knocking on the zinc roof that covered Nana's outhouse. This was the expected guest announcing his intention. Like an orchestra about to play a symphony, the tune up had ended, and the concert was just beginning. The full orchestration did not take long to strike up – actually within seconds there was a crescendo of sounds literally raining down on my ears. Mama and Papa had told me about this when I was younger, and now I was in it.

Raindrops like pebbles now played rather aggressively with the leaves. The sky was dark. I could see people running for shelter in the shop across the road. One man passed on a donkey going up the road. His shirt was already soaked, but the animal was moving like a bullet. Soon they were gone. I heard someone shout something from the shop across the road. I could not work out what was being said or who was saying it due to the sheet of rain between us. My mother described rainfall here as "rain to sleep by". I did feel relaxed. The house was eerily quiet but for the rain. I was sat on the veranda in Nana's most comfortable chair watching and listening. I lay back in the seat, and I must have dozed off.

I was awoken by the sounds of loud laughter and voices. I was startled. As I opened my eyes and focused, I could see and hear my Papa, Uncle Joe and my brother Jake. They were opening the grill to get on to the veranda. The rain had stopped, and the sun was out again. I had not heard the car pull up outside. I felt rested and relaxed as I got up and stretched.

"What wrong wid yu bwoy, yu grannie work yu hard today?" said my father.

"Not really," I said rubbing my eyes with the backs of my hands.

Uncle Joe and Jake were still laughing and joking as they entered the veranda with my dad. I was still a little dozy as Uncle Joe beckoned me closer to him. I had not seen him for many years, but he hadn't changed. I shook his hand.

"Soh yu just a go shake mi hand?" he said loudly.

As he said this, he grabbed and hugged me tightly. My uncle was really strong. He must have been about six feet four inches in height and almost as wide. He was built like a tank. Dad was not as tall, and he was slim. My father always said how much I resembled my uncle and now that I had grown I can see what he means. However, I'm not that wide – I am slim.

Papa said, "yu seh wat a tel yu, him big like yu".

Papa proudly looked at me from head to toe.

"No man", said my uncle, "him slim and mi stout. And mi taller than him to", said my uncle with a big grin on his face.

He had a gold tooth at the front of his mouth that glinted as it caught the sunlight which was high up in the sky once more.

"Taller dan wat", replied my father.

They bantered for a while and then proceeded to bring us together for comparison. On reflection, we were both about the same height, but my uncle still insisted that he was taller. They sat on the veranda and joked and laughed. My fifteen-year-old brother, who was almost six feet tall, sat next to me. Papa said that he will be taller than me when he grows up. I didn't think so. After all, he looked like Mama, and their side of the family are shorter. He looked tired so I asked whether he wanted to sleep and he said he did. He promptly lay back in the chair next to mine and dozed off within minutes. It seemed that it was not me alone that had a hard day. My father and uncle began telling me about their day in the town, shopping, the rain, the sun, and how I missed out.

Nana came out of the house and watched everyone talking and joking. She slowly sat in her favourite chair, unwrapped a mint and placed it in her mouth. Papa reflected on how well she looked. Nana smiled for a little while as she continued to survey the group of men that were gathered on her veranda. She even commented on Jake as he slept after all the walking that took place when then went into the town. One thing I know, Nana doesn't smile much.

However, it seemed like this was one occasion when a smile was worth it. She caught me looking in her direction, and the smile became a frown.

"Bwoy, wey yu a luk pon, goh fine something to duh!" she said suddenly.

She turned and went back into the house. I finished her smile. That's my grandmother, and I love her so much. A year later Nana passed away.

She was given a royal send-off fit for a queen. Papa and Uncle Joe spared no expense as they celebrated the life of an amazing mother and grandmother. I read the eulogy which ended: "...your words, your mannerisms, your expressions, always in my heart, forever".

Your loving grandson, Richie.

Three Long Years

Abraham, as was the case on most days when it never rained, was working in his field about a mile from home when the message was delivered. A young boy, who he did not recognise at first, came running towards him. Abraham's eyesight had never been good – and he needed new spectacles since he had sat on the last pair. The boy, who was around seven years old, seemed out of breath as he came closer, slowed down and walked the rest of the way, holding his side. Abraham knew straight away that something was wrong. So he stopped digging and dropped his fork on the red dirt of the slightly parched land he had inherited from his father. The boy was calling his name as he came up the hill.

"Uncle Abraham! Uncle Abraham!" he shouted.

Suddenly Abraham felt a sinking feeling in his stomach, much like when he knew that bad news was about to come his way. As the boy got closer, he realised that it was his nephew, Altman. He took a deep breath and braced himself for what he thought would be bad news. The last time he felt that way was when his father died, and they sent another boy to call him from the hills close to their home. On that occasion, he cried all the way home. Could it be Mama he thought? Visions of Clarabelle, his mother, who had not been well for some time, went through his head. She was a strong woman but of late she had suffered a series of illnesses which left her bedridden for weeks at a time. Abraham then considered whether it was one of his brothers or even the one sister he had left. Audrey, his eldest sister, died three years earlier from breast cancer that the doctors said was something else. They gave her all the pills under the sun, and none had worked. And all the time they had been taking every last dollar in her possession, ranted Abraham to himself. He was never able to trust doctors since that time. He felt a chill run down his back as his thoughts raced ahead of the news to come. Papa Ezekiel always told Abraham that he was never a patient man and that he needed a good woman to deal with that. He smiled a little but then realised that maybe it could be Papa Ezekiel. He then put it out of his mind.

Altman was now almost upon him. The boy was really tired and could not run anymore. Abraham decided to meet Altman, but as he tried to move, he noticed that his legs felt like jelly. So he quickly stopped, waited and instead shouted in the direction of Altman.

"Come, boy, come tell me what happen. And hurry!" shouted Abraham.

At first Altman, seemingly out of breath, could not get the words out. Then he managed, in between gulps of air, to finally say it.

"A Papa Ezekiel. Him dead!" shouted Altman.

Abraham sighed a little as if relieved that it was not his mother. Papa Ezekiel was one hundred and three years old! It was expected, he concluded. He had not been keeping the best of health over the past three years since his beloved Mama Eliza passed away and went to a better place to sing with the angels. Before that, he was as strong as a horse. Abraham hung his head in both sadness and prayer for a little while before again questioning Altman.

"Him really dead for true? When it happen?"

Altman, now getting back his breath, told him. "Yes. Just now! They find him dead in him a bed" said the boy now breathing more easily. "Grandma Rachel tell me to come tell you. She say you must come quick!" continued Altman.

Abraham immediately took up his work implement, raised it on to his shoulder, grabbed his bag and followed Altman as the boy turned to go back down the hill with Abraham not far behind him. "Careful boy, why you no sit down and get some rest first?

Altman did not hear him and was almost gone by the time Abraham reach far enough to see the road below. Although he had no spectacles, he could just make out the movement of Altman in the distance as he raced down the old road.

"One day, that boy going turn a good runner," Abraham said breathlessly.

Grandma Rachel was in tears. It had not been long since her mother, Mama Eliza, had passed. She had been sick for a long time, and Papa Ezekiel was devastated when she died. They had been together for eighty-five years. Since she went, on many occasions the family would hear Papa Ezekiel calling Mama Eliza's name and when she did not answer he would call everyone else to ask whether they had seen her. Over the years they had been the best of friends, went everywhere together, and there had never been a cross word between them for anyone else to hear. They were a perfect couple.

"Today," thought Abraham, "they will be jumping for joy together, wherever they are."

Then Abraham thought better about what he was thinking and instead uttered to himself "A sure they in Heaven cause they live so good and fear God".

Abraham sat on the veranda holding Grandma Rachel's petite hands in his own big shovel-like hands. She had raised Abraham since he was three years old until he became a man. He too had tears in his eyes and had that faraway look as if remembering all the good times with Papa Ezekiel. However, from the corner of one eye, he noticed that someone had come into the yard. He could not see well, and tried to wipe away the tears as he recognised Mary-Jane walking up the steps to the house. He had not heard her coming and was a little startled by her presence. Abraham turned to question her.

"You couldn't call when you come to the gate, Mary-Jane?" said Abraham.

Mary-Jane had already seen him wiping the tears away from his eyes.

"It okay for a man cry you know Abraham," she told him as he let go of Grandma Rachel's hand to open the grille door to let her into the house.

Inwardly, Abraham disagreed with what she had said. It was never manly to cry before a woman - except before Grandma Rachel.

"Mi no crying. What make you think so, the sun in my eyes" said Abraham with a big grin on his face.

However, Abraham's bravado did not last long as the tears kept on coming, and he turned his head away from Mary-Jane and tried his best to stem the flow. Mary-Jane gave him a wry grin at his pathetic attempts to impress her with his manliness. And yet she hugged him before she made her way over to Grandma Rachel and hugged her tightly for awhile.

"A just hear about Papa," she said slowly with sadness in her voice. "He was a good man with a loving heart, just like you, Grandma Rachel".

"Thank you me child," said Grandma Rachel."

Mary-Jane offered to help out any way she could, and Grandma Rachel thank her again. And then her tears came again. Mary-Jane took her hands and held them gently as she sat down next to the old lady who was more like a little girl who had lost her father. She needed a lot of reassurance and support, thought Abraham.

For three years Abraham had admired, and even loved, Mary-Jane, but he could never bring himself to tell her how he felt about her. She was the woman that he wanted more than any other, but he had always been too shy to approach her. Abraham's excuse always came to mind whenever he saw her. "What if she say no and make me look bad?"

It seemed like every time he saw her she did something to him that he just could not explain. And whenever she spoke to him and asked his opinion of anything, with those rolling eyes, he simply became tongue-tied and acted like a shy little boy. A shy little boy that loved a beautiful woman who he thought did not feel the same way about him. However, she had been waiting a long time for someone. Everybody had eyes for Mary-Jane, but she had eyes for nobody. Abraham could never understand that woman.

On the day of the funeral, the hearse carried Papa Ezekiel, with hymns blaring out from its loudspeakers, through the district and headed up the road to the old church. Everyone could hear the vehicle from at least a mile down the road. Abraham was already dressed extremely smartly and standing with other men outside the church as the coffin arrived. He and several others slid the coffin from out of the vehicle and carried Papa Ezekiel into his beloved church for the last time. Others followed behind the coffin as the hymn 'Precious Lord' could be heard playing from within the church. The coffin was lowered and secured at the front of the church and flowers were brought by the women to decorate it.

Some people were seated inside the church building, others were standing at the door, and a few of the latecomers and a couple of drunken men from the district stood outside in the hot sun. Abraham sat inside the church next to Grandma Rachel. It seemed like the whole district, and those on the outskirts too had come to pay their last respects to Papa Ezekiel. He was indeed a popular and well-loved man. Many people had come to help with the burial as a sign of respect for the great man. Indeed, some had come many miles, and there were minibuses and cars parked all along the narrow road.

When the speeches began, everyone had something good to say about Papa Ezekiel, and most people talked about his love for Jesus, the Bible and the church. Many remembered his challenges to them. Papa Ezekiel would say "Turn from your wicked ways and get right with God. No man knows when dem time will come to leave this sinful world". Papa Ezekiel knew how to turn a phrase, and few could touch him when it came to reciting the Word of God. He also knew when it was his time to go. Abraham remembered his last words to him. Papa told him that "No point you wait on man to give you anything. You have to go get it for yourself. And you must have the courage to do it."

Such wise words thought Abraham as he sat listening to the celebration that was Papa's life. He was so reflecting on those special times with him that he forget where he was as everyone else rose for another hymn. He was the last to rise and with no idea as to what hymn he was about to sing. Mary-Jane had been watching him. She just smiled. The funeral for Papa Ezekiel was one to behold. Altman was crying. Grandma Rachel was crying. Mary-Jane was in floods of tears. And, Abraham, who told everyone that a man must never cry in front of a woman, desperately tried to hold it back but cried like a baby. He was unable to hide those tears from Mary-Jane. Abraham cried the most and for the longest that day. And everyone came to sing, make music and spoke great words about Papa Ezekiel. Abraham also noticed some of the same people who just came for the free drink and food. It was always a sight to behold. He shook his head and had to smile.

Later, after the service, Papa Ezekiel's grandchildren and great-grandchildren carried the coffin to its final resting place - a lovely family plot on a hill that had a great view of the valley below. It was a long way to the place of rest, but everyone danced and sang all the way down the road, round the bend, up the old road, past Mother Smith old yard, across the rugged ground and finally up the hill to where the grave had been prepared. There was so much dignity in the way people behaved that day. Papa Ezekiel would have been proud to see it all. He was always a man of principles and disliked injustice, hatefulness, greed, vulgarity and disorganisation.

Abraham was so moved by all the outpouring of love, he had started to cry again. Mary-Jane was watching him from across the graveside. Abraham turned away to dry his tears. He felt embarrassed once again; even though the whole church had earlier seen him cry. But then it dawned on him that no one cared if he cried. "As a matter of fact it was Papa's day and not his," he concluded. Abraham shook off the self-consciousness, thanked Papa Ezekiel and proceeded to help the other people at the graveside as he was prayed for, sang to, lowered into the earth, covered with love by all and decorated. Everyone had a chance to say their last goodbye to a worthy saint. For Papa Ezekiel, it was a fitting tribute and send-off so that he could eventually be where he had always wanted to be - sitting by the right hand of God. He was buried next to his beloved Eliza. They were together once again, and they will be some dancing going on, thought Abraham.

After the funeral, Mary-Jane returned to the house with Grandma Rachel by her side and holding her hand. She called from the bottom of the steps for someone to open the grille door. Abraham, sitting on the veranda, got up to open the grille and greeted them both as they entered. He noticed that Grandma Rachel had stopped crying. And it seems as if they were sharing a joke together. Grandma Rachel went to put down her handbag.

"This time, you call before you come up!" Abraham said to Mary-Jane.

Mary-Jane simply nodded and smiled as she sat down close to Abraham, who seemed a little uneasy as she then went on to take a good, long look at him. He was not quite sure where to put his eyes. By that time Grandma Rachel had returned from inside the house to join them. She looked at them both for a long time before she spoke.

"Papa Ezekiel and Mama Eliza still with us," she said as she took both their hands, put them together and insisted that Abraham does the right thing by Mary-Jane.

Although a little awkwardly at first, they held hands for the first time. Mary-Jane smiled. And so did Abraham. It was all that they could do after three long years.

The River Bank

"Get up man, a time fi goh down a river. Unno noh get up yet?" cried Janie aiming her words at the large grilled and brightly painted dwelling just a little way up the road from her own rather basic two-bedroom house.

Janie's voice had cut deeply into the uncharacteristic stillness of the early and sunny morning silence. As if to echo her words, another shrill voice was immediately heard in the distance. Janie was in her mid-twenties, slim, attractive, with a dark complexion, wearing a red tee-shirt and a blue skirt that rode slightly above her knees.

As Janie strolled down the main road through the tiny district, there was the sound of a vehicle's horns in the distance. As the vehicle approached, Janie moved to the side of the road and turned her back to the direction from which it was to come. A thunderous sound could be heard as it rounded a corner with speed. The thumping bass-line ripped unceremoniously through the morning stillness as the vehicle, a taxi, filled with people, literally flew by Janie kicking up dust and dirt that had previously settled for the night.

"A mek dem man yah soh mad pon the road?" asked Janie as the taxi turned another corner and disappeared into the distance.

She never waited for an answer, but, after brushing down herself, continued her extremely slow progress up the road.

Dreams of Freedom

"Yu noh hear mi?" she turned and shouted once more.

From the house up the road, a quieter voice replied "Yes man, mi ready long time. Mi soon come".

Janie asked: "Wey Danielle, she noh ready yet?"

"Mi noh know," the other voice replied.

A little way up the road, Danielle, a plump and pleasant-looking young woman, probably in her mid-twenties, dark complexion, holding a young child by her side, opened a gate and came out of a small, unkempt house. She was wearing faded jeans with a white top.

"Yu know how long mi ready. A-ho!" said Janie as she stopped outside Annette's house.

Danielle proceeded up the road with the child hanging by her side. "Mi soon come," she said.

"Noh tan lang yu know, the driver soon come," said Janie.

Danielle just waved her hand and slowly meandered up the road, her slippers dragging on the dry road surface, much like a child with nowhere in particular to go.

Annette came out of her house. She was slim, of fair complexion, pretty, younger than the others, maybe in her early twenties, and wearing a long lime green frock with yellow flowers all over. She ambled towards the waiting Janie.

"Wen Peter coming'?" asked Annette.

"Mi tell him six-a'clack and a nearly six-thirty now," said Janie, and all the time looking down the road and setting her face like it was about to rain.

From where she was standing Janie could see two young men passing by and looking in her direction, wearing big grins and pointing at her. As they came closer, one spoke to Janie.

"Yaah come a dance tomorrow?" he asked.

"Deh answer is yes, but mi naah goh wid nun a yu!" said Janie with a serious and defiant look on her face.

Annette giggled, and the young men laughed out loud as they carried on up the road and at intervals looking back at the two women. Janie just kissed her teeth.

"Mek dem gwaan bout them business," she said to Annette, "dem man dere like too much gal-gal."

Janie noticed Annette's bags of washing by the roadside and quickly decided to go back to her house for her bags.

The driver, Peter, arrived at seven o'clock and pulled up by the side of the road, close to Janie's house, as leisurely as ever, and got out of the car. As he was leaning against the vehicle Janie came out of her house. She looked furious.

Dreams of Freedom

"Is wat time yu call dis?" she asked him as she stood hands akimbo as if ready for a showdown and her mouth similar to guns at the ready - cowboy-style.

Peter turned to face her. He seemed to be in his late twenties, over six feet tall, muscular in appearance, dark in complexion and wearing a navy short-sleeved shirt and black trousers. His shoes were well polished - a person would easily see their face reflected in them.

Peter just look at Janie and jerked his shoulders as if to say "no problem, I'm here now". However, it seemed as if that was not enough for Janie.

"Is wat time yu call dis?" she repeated the question but this time, she was more like a mother interrogating a child who had been late getting home.

Before Peter could say a word she continued, "Yu tel mi sey yu wi come at six-a'clack and yu jus a come."

Peter just smiled, groomed his beard with his hand while looking up the road where he noticed Annette and Danielle standing next to their respective houses with what seemed like bags of clothes to be washed and other items to be loaded into his car.

"Road bad yu know" replied Peter in a low but rather apologetic voice as he came around the side of the car to hug Janie. "And I had to mek a stop".

Before Peter could reach out to hug her Janie kissed her teeth and stepped away from him to lift her bags into the vehicle. Peter continued watching her and smiling to himself. Then Janie confronted him again.

"Soh wat, yu hand join church? Yu kyan help me?" she asked in a rather harsh tone.

Peter eventually assisted and began putting the various items into the boot of his car. Janie insisted on carrying some of the clothes with her in the back of the car. When they were done, Peter drove a little up the road to collect the other girls. He got out of the car to help Annette with her items. Danielle picked up and packed her clothes and other items by herself. Annette then sat in the front seat next to Peter. When they were all comfortably seated, he turned the car around and headed for the river.

Danielle and Janie, as was usual, were chatting loudly in the back of the car. Janie was still complaining about how long it had taken Peter to arrive, while Danielle was continually saying how hungry she was. She told them that she had had no breakfast and a small dinner the night before. Annette was merely looking out of the car window. She was watching people as they passed by on donkeys, bicycles and those who were simply walking by. She saw children playing as they were on their way to school or waiting for taxis to arrive.

Several vehicles passed them at speed and always blew their horns as they reached blind corners along the road. Some drivers never blew their car horns and one vehicle came around the corner and was surprised to see Peter's car. Peter had already blown his horn.

Peter shouted angrily at the driver who just waved and continued on his way. Janie was upset after the incident.

"Why some peeple soh mad pon the road?" she cried. "A good ting yu can drive Peter," she continued and tried to get a response from the others in the vehicle. Danielle and Annette were both quiet as the car slowed down for the old narrow bridge ahead.

Only Peter responded to Janie's comment. "People just want others to know dat they are there. Soh yu must blow yu horn. Some just a show-off and some reckless".

Peter, looking through his rear-view mirror, noticed Annette. He looked at her for a moment too long before their eyes met. The both smiled.

Peter was making good time on his way to the river when Danielle asked him to stop the car by a little shop. She fidgeted around in her pockets for some money, found some, quickly got out of the car and made a beeline for the shop. In no time at all, she returned eating a small bun. She then opened and began drinking soda just before Peter drove off.

"Soh yu noh get mi nuttin?" asked Janie.

"Yu did give mi money fi get yu sumting?" replied Dannielle as she tucked into the bun and drank the soda.

Janie looked at her as she continued eating and drinking. She was totally unconcerned with anybody else. A little further down the road, this time, it was Janie who asked Peter to stop the car. She smiled at him and exited the vehicle. She then came to the driver's side, leant on the door and spoke with him.

"A got sumting to give sumbaddy. A soon come," she said as she quickly turned around and walked away. Peter watched her as she walked away, and simply shook his head in disbelief.

She disappeared down a little embankment and returned a short while later. She was laughing and joking with another woman who had walked up the embankment with her. The two were in deep conversation before she eventually waved her goodbye, returned to the vehicle and the journey resumed.

A short distance down the road there was a sharp turn into a small gravelly road filled with holes. The road was on a steep hill going down towards the river. Peter was careful to inch his way down before speeding up along the flatter sections of the road. The girls were busily talking and at the same time keeping their eyes on the journey as he gradually descended the hilly road.

He was weaving from one side of the road to the other so as to find the best route through what could, in some cases, be extremely dangerous terrain for the vehicle's undercarriage, tyres or shock absorbers. On several occasions, the wheels unexpectedly entered presumably invisible potholes. Peter could see them coming, but sometimes they came two or three at a time and therefore gave the driver no chance but to enter at least one.

Peter's skill ensured that the vehicle continued undamaged. He came on to a straight in the road that was also very rocky. Other vehicles had obviously gone that way before since their individual tracks could be seen winding snake-like along the road. Many were able to drive up the side of the road to avoid the large rocks and others had taken a route on the opposite side of the road. Some had even gone over the rocks at the expense of damaging the underside of their vehicles. They suddenly hit a big pothole and another.

"Man, yaah goh kill wi? Yu shudda drive roun' de adda way," screamed Janie as they hit yet another pothole in what seemed like a wretched road.

"A yu a drive di car or a mi?" retorted Peter as he carefully picked his way along the road.

"Mek di man drive di car noh, Janie! Yu know seh di road bad a'ready", said Danielle.

Janie folded her arms and sat back in her seat.

"How yu know which way to goh?" asked Annette.

"When I was in the army I was trained to drive anywey and everywey. All cross the island. Day and night," replied Peter, as he went down in another pothole. "But some you kyan avoid."

It seems like Peter was still learning and occasionally remembered an important lesson. "My driving ability cannot be questioned," he said as he hit yet another pothole. The women in the back of the vehicle laughed loudly, while Annette looked at him and smiled. "Watch out for that one," cried Annette

Peter managed to avoid the pothole and turned his head to smile with Annette. Their eyes met once more. The others were watching intently from the back and nudging one another. Suddenly he hit another pothole. And everybody, including Peter, laughed.

Eventually, they reached the smooth road and saw a river crossing ahead, but Janie pointed out to Peter that they wanted to follow the river around until they reached an area where many people came to wash.

The riverbanks had an unwritten first come first use policy. The girls were looking ahead to see whether others had already arrived. Janie, who else, saw a car behind her and told Peter to drive faster. The road at this point was very narrow, a little muddy and dangerous. Peter paid her little mind because he knew that nobody could pass him. Janie was agitated and kept on looking behind her to see what was happening. The other vehicle was on their tail.

Nearing the riverbank, Janie asked Peter to stop the car, and he did. The women jumped out of the car, Janie with a basket she had been carrying, and Danielle and Annette each with a small bag of clothes. They each proceeded to run in front of the car. The vehicle behind them also stopped, and two other women were out and running towards the same riverbank. It was like a hundred metres dash at the island's athletics stadium. Peter was careful so as not to hit anyone especially as the women from the other car brushed against his and sprinted ahead of him. He slowed the car to a crawl and watched the race for the finishing line.

Janie was first to reach the riverbank, and she sat and waited for the others. The part of the river she had chosen gave easy access to the water, it was less muddy, and there were some rocks on which she could put washed clothes. The river was not deep at that spot, probably about four or five feet at most; and it was flowing quite slowly so that it was possible for people to swim or bath. Peter parked the car by the riverbank. The other "runners" – and losers - in the race had walked further up the river to find a new spot. People were washing on the opposite bank of the river. They had come from further down the parish. Peter and the victors, with their golden smiles, unloaded the car.

"Suppose yu did come later? Wi wudda miss dis spot," she said to Peter. He paid her no mind on that occasion. "A good ting a did get up early," she continued.

"Missis, yu shudda run fah Jamaica", said Dannielle to Janie as she sat proudly on the riverbank like a Nubian Queen on her ancient throne.

The women were washing and chatting amongst themselves so Peter went for a short walk up the riverbank. Janie was telling the other girls stories about her great-grandmother Sissy who used to wash in the river every Friday without fail. She told them how she was never sick and that she died of old age at ninety-five years old. Annette told them that her great-grandmother used to do the same thing and how, when she died, she had just returned from washing at the river.

"I never know any a mi grandparents," said Danielle. "My mother dead when I five years old, and mi aunt raise all of wi, and she never talk 'bout family," she continued rather sadly.

As they talked it became clear that the women had all grown up together in the district, and none had ever been to the capital, Kingston, and neither had they been to the north of the island.

Danielle said that she heard that all the people on the north coast were white, and they come from abroad.

"My aunt in England say that people noh wash a river. They have washing machine in di house and dey even dry clothes ina di house," said Janie. They all laughed at the image that Janie painted. "A where dey get sun fram in de house fi dry clothes?" asked Annette with mischief in her eyes.

They all laughed again. Janie then launched herself into a conversation she had with an aunt.

"My auntie also sey that people wear coat all di time because it soh cole. I asked my auntie wey she a duh a such a cole place. She sey the money gud". "I wud like to goh a farin, but I don't want to goh ina noh cole," she said shaking her head.

"A hea' sey sum part a farin noh cole yu know. A hea' sey Florida hot like Jamaica. I wud goh deh," said Danielle. "At least yu can dry yu clothes outa door", she continued.

Everyone laughed again. The women seemed to be in a dream world of their own making while washing their clothes. Annette was listening so intently and not paying attention to what she was doing that a piece of her washing almost got carried away by the river. Janie shouted her, and she had to move quickly to retrieve it. Janie and Danielle laughed loudly.

"A wat yu a tink bout soh girl, yu have a man?" said Janie laughing out loud again.

Peter returned from his walk.

"Wat yu fine round dey? Yu seh a woman yu like, and she run yu?" Janie joked.

Janie seemed to enjoy making fun of Peter because he would just laugh it off or just smiled and remained quiet. However, sometimes they both get into arguments – with Janie doing most of the arguing.

"Yu can talk stupidniss sometimes yu know," said Peter.

"Yu kyan tek a joke, eh man?" was Janie's reply.

The others just carried on with what they were doing, since they were used to the arguments between the two of them. Peter and Janie had known one another the longest – since schooldays when Peter would come to see his uncle who lived in the district. The argument continued between the two for a little while. But then Danielle, who wanted to stop them arguing, could hold it in no longer.

"Peter, how come yu noh have noh, woman? Sumting wrong with yu?" asked Dannielle.

She observed Peter's nervousness as he fumbled to find the right words to say. He seemed unprepared for such a question and looked at Annette before replying.

"A just noh fine di right woman yet," a smiling Peter replied.

"Soh wat bout Janie?" said Danielle looking at Janie for a reaction as she spoke to Peter.

Dreams of Freedom

Peter looked at Janie with a crazy look in his eyes that resembled revulsion, and she kissed her teeth and looked away. She resumed washing her clothes with gusto.

"Yu know sey unno always a quaaril like married people?" continued Danielle while looking from one to the other.

Peter looked in Janie's direction to see her response. She just continued with her washing.

"Mi noh want noh man wey so quiet. Dem sey silence river run deep", retorted Janie without raising her head from what she was doing.

"Danielle, how you like farce inna people business soh?" said Janie. Danielle looked at Janie, smiled, and continued her line of questioning, much like a lawyer in a courtroom.

"Wat kina woman yu a luk fah?" quizzed Dannielle.
"A suppose, sumbaddie like mi" he replied. Danielle looked at him quizzically. It seemed to her there may have been a question as to why he did not say somebody like her.

Peter noticed the look too and, for a moment, their eyes met. They both smiled. Annette looked away pretending not to hear the conversations taking place. The other girls had not noticed the eye contact between them.

It seemed to have been getting too hot for Peter and he decided to take another walk along the river bank. The river had many people washing on both banks. However, some people came to bathe. It was then that he noticed her. She was bathing a little way down the river and had decided to remove her top. She was almost naked as he took furtive glances in her direction. So that the others couldn't see what he was doing, he walked towards the car. The woman looked like someone in her mid-thirties, and Peter noticed how lovely she appeared. His passion was aroused as he watched. It seemed like he could not help himself. He looked back towards the women behind him, and he could see that they were busy washing and chatting. He particularly looked for awhile at Annette. His eyes revealed that something was stirring in his heart for her.

He turned to look at the woman bathing, and she suddenly looked in his direction. Immediately Peter turned away with a look of embarrassment on his face. He leant on his car with his back to the woman who was bathing and for a while, he was lost in his thoughts as he stared into space. He then returned to the real world where the girls were still talking. By the time he decided to go back to the girls on the river bank, he also noticed that the bathing woman had gone. But then he noticed that she had immersed herself in the river. He looked away once again but only to notice that Annette had caught sight of him. She stared at him for awhile as she continued to wash. The others noticed what they thought was going on. Peter smiled, turned and walked away along the road. Annette seemed disappointed as she turned to face the others.

"Yu like him?" asked Janie with excitement in her eyes.

"A don't tell yu that" replied Annette.

"Mi seh how yu jus luk at im. Yu fraid to sey yu like him?" enquired Danielle with a big grin on her face.

"I noh fraid nuttin. A tink a dah woman who a bathe over dere so im like," said Annette.

They looked at the woman who had been bathing, who was now swimming in the river and looking across in their direction. Peter had disappeared down the road. They looked at one another.

"Yu tink im like her?" said Janie.

"I know im like her. Yu shudda seh di way he did a luk pon her wen she a bade", said Annette disgustedly. "He noh have noh interest ina woman like me", she continued with even more disappointment in her voice.

"Any a yu know her?" asked Janie.
None of them had seen the woman before. However, they felt that maybe the woman was too old for Peter.

"She look like she much older than him," said Janie.

Annette took a good look at the woman and replied, "I don't tink sey Peter cud manage her", said Danielle.

"A soh mi a tink to," said Janie.

They all agreed that Peter would be better off with a younger woman. A woman that was quiet like him, with a nice smile, hard working, have no children and pretty. Danielle and Janie focused their attention back to Annette. Annette recognised what they were doing, looked away and continued washing.

Dreams of Freedom

Peter came back. It was almost midday. Everyone was hungry, and the washing was almost finished. Peter took out from the car the food that had been brought. The women had prepared some fried chicken, plantain, breadfruit and saltfish. Peter went for the beer and soda which he had earlier put into the river by the bank to cool. They all sat down to eat. Everybody was hungry, and the conversation was not too exciting until Janie brought up what Peter was doing earlier.

"A seh yu wen yu watching di woman a bade ina di river. Yu like her?" said Janie quietly.

"No man, a she did a watch mi," said Peter.

Danielle and Janie looked at one another as if to say 'a who im a try fi fool?'

"How yu mean?" asked Danielle.

"As me sey a she did a watch mi'," he said again.

"A she was the naked one or a yu?" enquired Janie.

Peter smiled and continued to eat his food, but took a quick glance at Annette. Annette did not even glance at him. Danielle and Janie noticed that Peter and Annette were not talking and took the initiative.

Janie turned to Danielle and said: "yu know, I tink sey Peter like sumbaddie, but a noh di woman did a bade".

She spoke just loud enough for Annette and Peter to hear, but talking as if neither of them was close by.

"Yes, a soh mi tink to", chipped in Danielle.

"Yu know a who he like?" asked Janie mischievously.

Janie was pointing by pouting her lips in Annette's direction. Annette was not looking and just continued eating and seemingly with no interest in their conversation. Peter was doing the same thing too – his attention was probably elsewhere. But Janie and Danielle could see signs of uneasiness coming from them both. So they continued.

"Mi seh di way dem luk pon one anada. Dem noh want admit it but mi seh it. Yu know wey mi a sey?" said Janie.

Danielle agreed with Janie. Peter looked up.

"A mi unno a talk bout soh?" asked Peter.

"If dah cap fits..." said Janie as she looked at Dannielle, who in turn was observing Annette's reactions.

Neither Peter nor Annette said another word. Each continued eating and not looking in either one's direction. The silence was awkward. Peter finished eating and got up from the group. Annette went back to her washing.

For a time Annette seemed rather perturbed and was not joining in with any of the conversations between the other women. She occasionally looked up from what she was doing and smiled at the others. Peter washed up the dishes and utensils that they had used, stored them away and stood by the car whistling a tune. He seemed all unconcerned with his surroundings as he looked across the river. He appeared to be a little agitated.

Some time later a young man came running toward them. He seemed tired because he was panting and sweating. He came up to the group out of breath.

"Hide mi man, hide mi noh? A man out fi kill mi dead" said the youth with great fear and foreboding in his voice.

Peter came running to see what was going on. Janie was looking around to see if anyone else was coming after the young man. Danielle and Annette looked shocked and afraid. Then there were more footsteps and another youth running toward and brandishing what seemed like a gun. Annette and Danielle suddenly drew back and toward the car. Janie stood on the riverbank. Peter was standing in front of the young man who was cowering and pleading with them to hide him. The gunman saw him, stopped running and slowly walked over toward Peter.

"A gwine kill yu backside, bwoy. Mi want mi money," said the gunman.

He came closer, lifted the gun and pointed it toward the youth who was still cowering and whimpering behind Peter. Peter stretched out his hand toward the young man with the gun.

"Just calm down noh man. Tell mi what a gwaan," pleaded Peter. The women knew that Peter had his Military training and experience, but they were not sure what that really meant. There was fear in Annette's eyes. Danielle ran and hid behind the car. Janie stood just across from Peter.

"yu noh gwine get nuttin fram im if yu kill im?" stated Peter. The gunman then decided to point the gun at Janie.

"Wat yu know, keep outa man affairs, a im mi come fah? Im gwine dead todeh!" he said to Janie.

"Wah im do soh bad?" asked Peter.

"Im tief mi money" shouted the gunman.

"Anno mi tek it. A yu brada. A im tek it!" shouted the youth courageously and still cowering behind Peter.

The gunman seemed to have become even more agitated at the accusations made by the youth.

"Yu lie!" he shouted angrily, "get ready fi dead, bwoy. Come outa di way mek mi murder im now," screamed the gunman.

The youth remained hidden behind Peter. And Peter decided not to move. Neither did the youth. Peter asked the gunman to check out whether the youth's story was true. The gunman insisted that his brother could not have double-crossed him. Janie asked the man to listen to Peter and try what he said. The gunman insisted that that could not be. Peter asked him whether his brother was nearby. The gunman stated that he was up the road waiting for him. Peter requested that he go to get him, and he would hold the youth until he returned. Peter firmly grabbed hold of the youth. The gunman seemed uncertain at first but eventually lowered his weapon a little.

"Yu seem like yu mean it. But if yu a tel lie, a gwine hunt yu down and kill yu backside to" said the gunman to Peter in a threatening voice.

Peter insisted that he would keep his word. The gunman tentatively moved away walking slowly backwards until he was at a distance to run toward where he had come from. Peter held on to the youth and quizzed him to find out more.

He said that the gunman was his sister's boyfriend, and the other man was the gunman's brother. He said the brother was brought up in Kingston and had only recently come back to the district. He did not know the brother too well, but the brothers had become close since meeting. The gunman, he said, had always been good to him until his brother came on the scene. Peter recognised the situation as one that he had dealt with in the past while in the army.

"I deal with dis kinna situation before, and you just have to do what a sey," stated Peter.

The youth, through his crying and tears, agreed.

Danielle had left the safety of the car and drew closer to Janie. Annette drew closer to Peter while he was questioning the youth. Janie stood in a defiant mood. She wanted to know why the gunman had to point a gun at her face. She was using choice swear words at this time. Before Peter could answer the gunman returned and this time his brother was with him.

"Soh yu still have im here? Yu lucky! Seh mi brada here. Mek we tek di bwoy now!" said the gunman.

"Where is the man's money?" Peter asked the brada.

"Wey yu a ask mi fah, seh di bwoy wey, tek it deh," said the brother in a rather shaky voice.

"Dat man have yu money," said Peter to the gunman with some confidence.

"Wey yu a sey", shouted the gunman and waving the gun in Peter's face. "A mi brada dis. How yu know sey di bwoy noh have mi money?"

"Check im pocket, and yu weh fine yu money", replied Peter.

Derek began to wave the gun around again and pointing it at Peter. "If yu wrong, yu dead," he said in an unforgiving voice.

He asked his brother to see his pockets. At first, he refused and stated that Peter was trying to turn him against his own brother. The gunman was not convinced.

"Yu know dis man", asked the gunman to his brother, as he pointed at Peter.

The brother answered "no".

"Then mek mi seh yu pocket dem" the gunman insisted.

The brother could not get his words out. He started to sweat. His face was a picture. Derek pointed the gun at him and demanded that he saw what was in his pockets. As he emptied his pockets, Derek was shocked to see the amount of money that was being revealed. He checked some notes and agreed that that was his money. He moved his brother to where he could see him.

"Soh, yu come try an tief mi? Wey mi duh to yu? Said the gunman to his brother. "Yu nearly mek a innocent bwoy get dead," he continued.

"It mek sense now. A yu fi dead. Listen leave here now before mi change mi mine and kill yu backside. Gwaan!" shouted the gunman. The brother, walking backwards, tripped over a stone. He got up slowly, then turned and ran for his life – stumbling several times before he was out of sight.

"Get far awey fram mi. Far far!" shouted Derek after him.

Peter breathed a sigh of relief.

As he let go of the youth Annette grabbed hold of Peter's hand – she had fear and tears in her eyes. The gunman took the youth and escorted him away in the direction he had come.

"If mi seh him again mi gwine kill im dead" hollered the gunman. "Len mi di gun and I weh kill him fi yu", said the youth quickly regaining his confidence.

"No! Yu weh gaah prison. Gwaan home before mi lick yu ina yu head side" said the gunman.

Janie just sat down on the riverbank and breathed a huge sigh of relief. Danielle emerged from behind the car with tears in her eyes too.

"Janie, a tink a wet misef", she said.

Janie looked at her from head to foot and back again. Peter hugged Annette. Annette hugged him back. Janie decided to go over to comfort Danielle – and herself. Some clothes remained wet as everyone returned in silence to their homes that afternoon. And yet, both Peter and Annette may look back one day and realise that everything happens for a reason.

The Taxi Driver

Darkness was just a whisker away, and this could be seen in the number of car headlights that came down the road. The taxi driver, who had only at the last second saw the shadowy figure standing by the roadside, narrowly missed running into an oncoming vehicle but skilfully swerved and quickly screeched to a halt. Although a little annoyed he was glad for the fare since he had had a poor day.

The driver was twenty-something, stockily built, dark in complexion, with a small moustache and ruggedly handsome in appearance. The new passenger seemed middle-aged, not very tall and with a slightly receding hairline. As the man entered the taxi, he uttered a quick goodnight to everyone and sat in the backseat next to two young women. They both turned to look at the new passenger and then looked at one another. One woman suddenly started to shiver, said that she was cold and asked for the vehicle's air conditioner to be turned down. The driver told her that it was not on. Earlier, when picking up the man, the driver had noticed a vague familiarity.

As the driver slowly moved off there was an eery kind of silence but for the slightly subdued sound of the vehicle's radio playing Bob Marley's "No Woman No Cry". The driver was mouthing the words to the song as they drove past several roadside shops. As the darkness came down, the silence continued apart from further songs by Luciano, Buju Banton and Shaggy. The driver was fully concentrating on the road ahead as he flicked his headlights on and off to make out the road ahead and to let other drivers know that he was on the road. On several occasions, he had to use his horn to warn other drivers about their road manners. Sometimes he would mutter something under his breath and at other times he would let the passengers know how crazy some drivers were on the road.

Eventually, a small voice in the front seat of the vehicle was heard: "one stop driver".

This was a young schoolgirl carrying what seemed like a schoolbag. After letting off the young girl and collecting the fare, the driver preceded up the road for a short time until the two young women had also been decanted. The taxi driver had an eye for one of the young women and, as he watched her leave the vehicle, shouted: "Next time Angela". The young woman turned around, giggled and then turned to look at the other young woman. The vehicle continued on its way towards Old Harbour.

The May Pen to Old Harbour route was usually well travelled. However, since the opening of the new highway the traffic down the old road had lessened. Those drivers who did not want to pay the toll charged, or could not pay it, continued to use the route. It had always been a bumpy ride as the road was not well-maintained and sometimes this made it quite dangerous for some drivers. Many lives are lost on Jamaican roads each year, and the route was no exception. The last fatal accident that the taxi driver knew about took place about a month before when a man and his son were killed while driving along the same stretch of road. The accidents were usually caused by some people driving too fast and others overtaking along stretches of the road that were badly sign-posted. The taxi driver was driving quite fast as he continued his journey. And there was still a long way to go to reach Old Harbour.

Dreams of Freedom

The man in the backseat had been quiet throughout up to that point, and the driver peeked at him as he drove more slowly through a built up area. Taxi drivers sometimes grew nervous when they had lone passengers in the backseat. He was looking out for and hoping that another passenger would flag down his vehicle. But it was not his night for fares. Suddenly, the man started to talk. He begun by pointing out the dire state of some roads in Jamaica and considered that the government needed to set road safety as a priority as so many people were needlessly dying. The taxi driver agreed and listened for awhile as the man continued to talk. Somehow the man's voice was also vaguely familiar to him.

"It look like you know the road well around here", stated the man. The taxi driver nodded and let him know that he spent many years living in the area.

"How long you been a taxi driver?" asked the man. The taxi driver answered that he had been doing the job for three years.

"You seem like an intelligent young man, why you driving taxi?" asked the stranger.

The taxi driver told the man that he needed to make money to look after his family. "The most important thing to me is to look after my family. My father never did that. I make it my solemn duty to never be like that good-for-nothing man. A my goal that."
The stranger seemed quite uncomfortable as the taxi driver mentioned the words 'good-for-nothing man.'

He then went on to ask the driver about his family. The taxi driver told him about his young family. "I have a son aged four and a daughter aged two. And my wife is just like my mother. She so loving and care for everyone. We married five years."

The man was visibly emotional on hearing the young man talk about his family in such glowing terms. The driver asked whether he was okay and the man just nodded.

At that point, the driver had to concentrate on avoiding a passing motorist who had kept on his full headlight beam as they rounded a dangerous and narrow corner of the road.

"You see how these people use road bad!" exclaimed the driver.
The stranger agreed and commented, as before, about the state of the roads and added that some drivers were openly inviting the death and destruction on themselves. The driver suddenly felt a chill as he reached over to turn off the air conditioner and realised that it was already turned off. He nervously kept an eye in his rear view mirror to find any expression on the face of the stranger.

A short time later the stranger asked the driver about his ambition and whether he was going to drive taxis all his life. The driver was a little cross at the question but answered anyway.

"I now own two taxis and another man drive for me. Sometimes I hire out to tourists because I get more money," replied the driver.
The man seemed impressed as he nodded his head in agreement.
The driver continued. "I then want to buy a minibus and own a fleet. I want my own transport business, and right now I studying business too."

The stranger physically applauded the driver for his plans and then told him ruefully, "I wish I did do that when I was younger. My father left me when I was young too." The older man proceeded to tell the driver stories about his own childhood and the other children with whom he had grown up. The driver listened intently. Then the older man wanted to know where the younger man came from, and he responded and told him he was from Chapelton. The stranger told him that he was also from Chapelton.

"You come from Chapelton too? That's where I was born," said the driver excitedly. He continued, "Maybe you know my mother."

But before the driver could mention her name the older man responded, "Yes, she come from near Summerfield."

The driver looked quizzically through his rear view mirror at the stranger and asked: "How you know that?"

The man quickly replied that it was just a lucky guess. The driver was not too sure the man had given him a satisfactory answer. However, he continued to focus on his driving as it was now too dark to take any crazy chances. But fairly soon the man began talking about the young man's own life. He felt that only he and his family knew some of the things that he told him about. The man knew that he almost died when he was a baby, and he told him about the steps his mother had taken to keep him alive during those difficult times for the family. The driver knew most of what the man was telling him because he had spent many hours talking with his mother. The man even described his mother down to her very unusual laughter when she became excited over some things. How did he know so much? Thought the driver. He had begun to wonder about the true identity of the man he was talking to. He was thinking about how the man knew about his family's business.

The driver was still a grief-stricken son. The man noticed this and asked whether he was thinking about his mother to whom the driver told him he was and recounted the story of her battle with cancer and death. As he told the story tears came to his eyes. He drove while wiping the tears away. He then noticed that the stranger seemed to be crying too. He too was wiping away tears. The driver inquired as to whether the man had known his mother, to which he simply replied "yes" and mentioned her by name. The man told the driver that his mother was an exceptional woman who loved her children very much. The driver, now intrigued, wanted to know how the man knew his mother. To this question, the man told him that they attended school together and even dated for a while. The driver was amazed by the man's revelation and as they talked the driver was becoming more and more convinced that he knew the man that he was talking to, and he wanted to ask his name. The man then stated that the driver's mother had chased away men in her life because of her first love. However, this was something the driver did not want to hear about his mother and quickly accused the man of meddling in his family's affairs without knowing all the facts.

Before the young man could ask any further questions the man asked one of his own. "What did they tell you about your father?"

The driver hesitated a little before angrily stating what he had been told. "Mother said that father left because he couldn't deal with the responsibility of a family and go from one woman to another."

The stranger noted the anger in the driver's voice and wanted to know why that was the case. The young man, after a deep breath, replied, raising his voice a little more than before.

"I angry because he left us to fend for ourselves." The driver paused a little before continuing. "He decide to run around with other woman like a coward."

"What they say happen to your father?" asked the stranger.

The driver answered promptly. "My aunt say that he die in a road accident. He had a young son with him that die too."

The driver told the man that the accident happened on the May Pen to Old Harbour road, the one on which he was now driving. The driver looked ahead expressionless as he told the man, who seemed a little emotional as the driver tried to look at him through his rear view mirror - in between the oncoming lights entering his vehicle as they passed. The man was so familiar he thought the driver. For one moment he matched his own looks to the man and realised how much they looked alike and wondered whether he was the long lost uncle that his mother had talked about over the years.
The driver continued and told the man that his mother said his father was a worthless man who never cared for his son, and yet she always loved and defended him whenever other people told her anything negative about him. The man smiled to himself as he heard the words. Even with the anger, he had tried to find his father after his mother had died but he could not be found.

The stranger said, "I am sure that your father would have helped you if it was a life or death situation. No father is so bad he won't do that for his children".

The young man then revealed his true feelings and said, in a raised voice and aggressively, "Dem deh man dis fi dead bad".

The stranger, after allowing the driver to calm down, told him that fathers have to make difficult choices too. He told him that everybody made mistakes which they may eventually regret. However, he said, at the time it seemed like the right thing. Part of the problem, he added, was that many men did not know how to be fathers since they were never taught how.

"Why you making excuses for bad fathers?" asked the driver, "maybe you're one of those bad fathers I hear about. Just like my own father."

The driver's anger returned so much so that the stranger reminded him to keep his eyes on the road. He calmed down a little and reduced his speed. He then went on to tell the stranger about the life his mother ended up living as a result of what his father had done. "She died a year ago and regretted what she had put us through. That was painful to me because she did nothing wrong." The passenger listened intently to the young man's words.

"Fathers must be there for their children no matter what, no excuse," stated the driver forcefully.

The older man then said that the younger man's anger should fall at the feet of his mother since she had the opportunity to change things and take back his father. At that point, the driver wanted to stop the vehicle and threatened to eject the stranger unless he remained quiet for the rest of the journey. The older man kept quiet for a time.

Eventually, the driver could take it no more and had to get to the bottom of what he really wanted to ask. "Who are you?"

Dreams of Freedom

As the driver finally asked the all important question, the stranger avoided it and instead warned the driver about an accident ahead. The driver looked ahead and could see nothing and wondered what the man was actually saying to him. He uttered a few curse words under his breath. The man continued by stating that the accident had not happened as yet but it would soon. The driver started to get angry with the stranger and asked him whether he was some prophet or even God to know such things. The stranger was quiet at that point as the driver continued to rant and rave and disbelieved what he had said. However, the driver calmed down a little and reflected in quiet thought about what the man had already told him.

How could he know so much about him and not even know about him? He wondered. Only his parents would know such things, and he was sure that his father had known nothing about him. Anyway, the wretched man was dead he continued. So who was this man telling him such crazy things? He thought, with puzzlement on his face.

Suddenly, the man asked to be let out of the vehicle. As the vehicle stopped safely by the side of the road, and before the stranger could leave the car, two other vehicles passed at high speed. Both were heading in the direction of Old Harbour and both proceeded to overtake another vehicle which had earlier been in front of his taxi. A few seconds later there was the awful sound of screeching tyres and a horrific and almighty crunching sound. Twisting metal could be heard before there was an eerie silence. There had been an accident. Screaming and raised voices came from the direction of the accident. The taxi driver looked with astonishment in the direction of the accident before turning to the stranger standing next to his vehicle. The stranger at first grimaced at what he knew to be carnage up ahead, then smiled and walked away and up a small incline next to which there was an old and badly wrecked vehicle.

At that point, the taxi driver realised why the man was so familiar. They had the same smile; he noticed that they were both short and stocky, and he walked slowly and deliberately - just like he did. They even had the same wry smile, he thought. Then the sudden truth of the matter came to him. It was his father! However, the thought left his head as he remembered that his father had died. Immediately, the taxi driver then noticed the wreckage of the vehicle toward which the stranger had gone and realised what could have happened. By this time the man had disappeared. The taxi driver had a crazy thought that the stranger had not even paid his fare.

Still mesmerised by the spot where the man had disappeared, he thought how lucky he had been and how much his father really must have cared for him - even if from the other side. He allowed a nervous smile to appear on his face before he turned and ran towards the scene of destruction that had occurred.

Epilogue

Linford Sweeney was born in Sutton's District near Chapelton, Clarendon, Jamaica in 1956, and came to the UK with his mother to join his father in 1964. He left school with minimal qualifications and worked in a factory before becoming disillusioned and re-entering full-time education to study business and management.
Since leaving full-time education, he has worked within the arts and entertainment industries, marketing in local government, training, lecturing, community development and the civil service.

Furthermore, for over forty years he has been an active volunteer in community work and co-founded several groups, including the world famous and once vibrant Nia African Cultural Centre in Manchester.

Today, Linford Sweeney is the founder of **Inspired Histories** and develops and delivers African-Centred history education, family history research and other cultural and heritage programmes. He is the author of 'At Peace With Myself' and several e-books (Muhammad Ali, Nelson Mandela, Black contributors to Britain's history).

He is currently working on his next book, The African Spirit, a collection of poems and stories aimed at raising African consciousness.

Services

To access Linford Sweeney's services which include Jamaican family history research, black history courses and presentations and developing cultural/heritage projects, he can be reached at inspiredhistories@gmail.com, or you could visit www.inspiredhistories.com, to purchase these services.

Linford Sweeney is also an experienced Life and Spirituality Coach (helping people to build their confidence, to grow spiritually and mentally). He published his first book, *'At Peace With Myself: An Affirmations Workbook'*, in 2011 and this is still available from Amazon or preferably by emailing inspiredhistories@gmail.com.

Linford is quite happy to receive feedback from readers about the book, and he can be contacted at the above email address.

Lightning Source UK Ltd.
Milton Keynes UK
UKOW05f0153231116
288257UK00011B/231/P